Praise for M.A. Harper's work:

"The romantic plot is sweet, hot and well-paced ... quiet but momentous scenes of growing affection create a deep-down satisfying novel."

—*Kirkus* Reviews

"There's a genuine ghost story here, but it's the human story that sets off shivers."

—*San Francisco Chronicle*

Fire on the Bayou

Book Two,
The *Jolie Blonde* Series:
A Louisiana Trilogy

BY

M.A. Harper

booksBnimble Publishing
New Orleans, La.

Print ISBN: 978-0-692324158
eBook ISBN: 978-0-9904543-3-5

www.booksbnimble.com

First booksBnimble publication: October, 2014

Print layout by eBooks By Barb for Booknook.biz

CHAPTER ONE

The woman who foresaw his death wasn't the same one he happened to be in love with.

That was Mickey, nick-named back in high school by A.P. himself. The love of his life, people would remember, but not the person predicting the tragedy.

Delphine. She was the one.

Who'd been glimpsing it for years from the corner of her eye, the gradual self-destruction homing in on him like a stalker, an inevitable result of bad habits and carelessness taking so long to get here that she could almost suppose it never would. What finally kicked her concern into high gear as the 1980's drew to a close were these nightmares she'd begun having—Our Lady of Lourdes full of flowers, people weeping and speaking A.P.'s name, she spotted family members in the pews and heard solemn organ music. But with him never among them. Nowhere visible.

Dreams don't have to mean anything, she told herself, waking up in yet another icy sweat on yet another dark morning, Paul snoring beside her. *Like, before we lost Tee-Nick, did I dream anything important? No. I would've remembered. Your little boy burns himself to death, you remember every single thing. Even if you don't want to.*

But it got to where she finally had to face it, hanging up her apron one October weekend to catch the next Greyhound bus for

Slidell. Because if God planned to wrest another son from her, He'd have to fight like hell to get it done.

* * *

She took her own reserved place out front. And then had to reposition her chair as far away from the people at the next table as she could get, its metal legs scraping across the concrete floor. *I don't need to hear your commentary, y'all. Been a long time since I saw him perform, but if he sucks, I'll know it without anybody's help.*

The place was filling up now. Getting loud.

"This is for you." A.P.'s manager/sound man/whatever brought her a draft beer.

What a pleasant surprise, no need to summon the waitress. Delphine groped around in her purse for her wallet. "You're an angel, Mr. Bee-Bee—how much I owe you?"

"Nothing."

"Well, I sure do thank you kindly."

"Come out your son's share," he shrugged. There was a lot of him to do it. He wasn't freakishly tall, exactly—no more than six-foot-five—but broad from the shoulders all the way down. And very black. He wore an eyepatch, but smiling didn't make it move because he never smiled. "You want something to eat, Miz Savoie? Bad food here, greasy, but it'll fill you up. Burger or po'-boy…"

She shook her head. "I ate on the bus. But thanks."

He nodded, still unsmiling. And then made his way to his place in the back.

Maybe he's wondering why I'm here. If he asked me, what would I say?

* * *

Guitar on his thighs like a folkie's, A.P. sat onstage atop a bar stool while two musicians at bass and keyboards made inaudible observations behind him. Delphine just had to shake her head at white skin showing through torn denim at his knees, that movie-star face of his masked by black beard stubble. *Maybe this is the*

Grunge look, what I've been reading about. But you'd think he'd get around to shaving, just once in a while. You'd think Bee-Bee would at least make him comb his hair, she glanced over her shoulder at the hulking silhouette back there.

The hulk gave a nod.

Didn't matter whether A.P. had all his fingers or not. He could still hold a pick, and his guitar rang like a bell.

Delphine had heard him sing since he could crawl, but this was different. Voice huskier now than she remembered, its lower register deeper. But still pitch-perfect on the high notes, even resonant—or was that mostly Bee-Bee's talent with a sound board? "Baby, we lived / In a wed-locked cage / With a love grown cold / And mutual rage…"

Used to be all rock or swamp-pop. All those dance halls and lounges he played at with Paul's brother. What kind of music you call this?

"…Like strangers now / Falling into the trap / Of my-fault, your-fault / Same ol' crap…"

Okay, so maybe he wrote this himself. I know who it's about, too. Definitely Mickey Wickham.

Her mug had no more beer in it. She signaled the waitress for another, eyeing the few other older women in the place. Delphine was petite and attractive, but in her fifties now, and needed nobody to remind her of it. The best-looking women here had frizzy hairdos, but hers was just a lank ponytail. *At least I'm skinny—*

Coo, was he standing? What was he doing off the stool? Limping around up there with a guitar strapped onto him, with no real balance, no one to catch him? She wasn't near enough to catch him, should he fall off the stage. She wasn't big enough to catch him.

She couldn't imagine anybody wanting to watch a disabled guy dance. Had Bee-Bee known he was going to do this?

The song made his features bunch up with the effort of getting it all out, every flayed emotion. Delphine was freaked. This was too private, this pain did not seem feigned, and he shouldn't put it on display like this. She set her beer back onto the table, but didn't get the mug all the way over the edge. It fell off. Cold liquid foamed down her leg, into her shoe.

"I made you suffer, girl, I made you cry / Blue holy eyes like a thunderstorm sky..." The amplified whisper was so quiet now that she heard her own nose whistling.

"Thick black night is the penance I done." He collapsed onto his knees with no warning, guitar hanging idle from strong shoulders. The *boom* of bone on the plywood was like the dropping of a scaffold trapdoor.

Gripping the mike, he raised his head and suddenly brayed " 'I'd walk a million miles for one of your smiles,' " in a perfect Al Jolson imitation that brought on nervous titters from several drunken women seated near the wall.

He spoke: "Except I can't."

The titters stopped.

"Hey, you married?" He made sudden eye contact with the plumpest one.

Embarrassed, she shook her head no.

"Spoken for?"—asked with high dimples denting the tops of his cheeks, raised straight brows, the flash of good teeth. *Handsome as hell, and I know I'm biased. But even that beard can't hide it.*

Scattered laughter sounded from far dark corners. Again came her negative.

"So can you assist me in something here, babe? Like lying down?"

Loud laughter. He too cracked up, wheezing into the mike. Then raised a palm. "No no no—didn't mean it that way, y'all. Don't mean for *her* to lie down. Unless she just wants to..."

Inaudibly, she responded and he cupped an ear. Merrily beckoning.

She crept hesitantly onstage to lusty cheers, conferred with him for a second, then helped him off his knees and onto his back— becoming an instant celebrity. The applause was deafening, her joy absolute. No doubt he could've done it without her, but this way made it entertaining, Delphine realized. A plus, not a minus.

He lay there on the floor, his little gold earring glittering in the stage light, and did Chuck Berry's *You Never Can Tell* in a tempo so rapid, under circumstances so bizarre, that Delphine couldn't think anymore. Her brain shorted out.

The nearby table began to shriek "*Awright! Aw right!*"

She covered her ears, then covered her mouth with one hand. A.P. didn't grow up singing like this, performing like this. This wasn't how famous people did it on television, flat on their backs, arms spread wide so that they looked like crucifixes.

Can't take your eyes off him.

Falling silent, he dropped the mike.

The Saturday night audience made a noise like a 747.

Would he be killing 'em this way, Delphine marveled in the happy din, *if he'd never met that girl named Mickey?*

Would he be killing himself?

CHAPTER TWO

What Mickey Wickham first loved about Terry Lanzl when she was introduced to him at a West Village cocktail party six months ago was how focused he seemed on every word she said and every move she made. He leaned in, intent, and made her feel fascinating. Well, she'd brought everything she had, which her mirror told her was considerable. Long legs, natural blondness, pale cleavage, great face. By one A.M., she wanted him to touch her. He took her home, touched her roughly, and it was... athletic. The Ironman Triathlon of sex. She was his sea for swimming, the uneven terrain to be crossed.

He didn't smoke, drank fine wines and then only at dinner, and took exemplary care of himself. The fact that he was younger was gratifying to her ego—*I'm still hot!*—with his powerful body like an action figure's, although that reddish hair was already beginning to thin a little. Thoroughly plugged into the metropolitan sports scene, Terry was Executive Assistant to The General Manager of the New York Jets and took advantage of exciting perks like the gym and sports medicine. *Whereas I don't get enough exercise,* she acknowledged, trying to walk all the way to the NYU Anthropology Department on the days she wasn't running late and had to take the subway. *I'm going to lose him if I gain any weight.*

And sometimes, I think the only person Terry's ever been in love with his whole life is Terry...

Another plus—of course—was that Cam seemed to like him. Cam hadn't had a positive reaction to most of the men she'd dated before this, but he was older now. Maybe able to understand a little bit better. Through therapy, something his mother tried to believe in, rationality she was willing to pay for with her trust fund from her father. Plus sought for herself, as well.

Terry cares for me and is protective. Anybody laying a hand on me, he'll break his arm, that's for sure. He says he will, and no doubt it's the truth. He loves being physical.

Terry's dependable. Educated. Father's a stockbroker.

Still...

He was gone a lot, at Jets headquarters, to famous restaurants with team staffers, to away games, and then he spent such a huge amount of intense time on the phone, even in her presence. Maybe things'd calm down in the NFL off-season, but she wasn't sure. He wasn't living with her. They hadn't had time yet to work out who'd move in with who, if indeed this turned out to be a serious relationship. Both of them had very nice places in decent buildings with doormen. *But whenever we mention it, Terry and I, he seems to automatically think he's going to move in here with me. Like, does he covet my apartment?*

Can he get to the Meadowlands easier from here?

"Hire a better cleaning lady, would you?" he'd object to the way chores were left undone—unimportant things, and Mickey was baffled. Little nickel-shit stuff made him angry. He preferred to call her "Michelle", and he did it like he owned her.

She lay beside him in bed now, exhausted by the lengthy and heated telephone conversation he was having with somebody—after beginning the season with high hopes, the Jets were tanking—and she wondered where she'd gone wrong. *Or maybe right, I don't know yet. Maybe he's good for me. My therapist thinks he is.*

He's conscientious. Eats organic. Behaves appropriately.

Still...

As God is my witness—no matter how wonderful Terry is—sometimes I can't help thinking about Adrien Paul Savoie and wishing it was his own worthless head still lying on my other pillow.

CHAPTER THREE

"Well, they're calling you 'The Cajun David Byrne'," Delphine told him as they pulled out of the motel parking lot the next morning. "Don't know if I like that, or not..."

He laughed. " 'Cajun' hasn't been a pejorative for decades, Feen."

"I still don't have to like it. And who the hell's David Byrne?"

"Front man for the Talking Heads—long story—who's saying this?"

"Article in a little weekly here." Her plucked brows arched as she scanned it. "Says you got 'pheno-'... 'phemom-'... Damn, I can't ever say that word right: 'Phenomenal'...?"

"Yes. Okay."

"Says here you also got better pipes than Byrne, whatever that means. 'Immensely entertaining, Savoie's originality defies easy categorization.' Hah!"

"I'll take that as praise..." He merged into traffic on I-10.

The amps and microphone stand in the back of the van slid in the shallow curve. Delphine turned to reposition her overnight bag closer to the guitar case, then felt a slight impact.

"*Shit!*" A.P. cut the wheel towards the shoulder and braked. Glanced into his side view mirror.

"What happened?"

"Hit a dog." He got out.

She turned, alarmed, glancing into the mirror on her side, then opening her door. There was a small dark lump yards up the Interstate behind them, A.P. making for it, a dangerous place to be going with only his cane to help him. *Dammit, son! I love dogs myself, but I'm not getting killed for one!*

Maneuvering herself over to the driver's seat, she backed the idling vehicle up the pull-off lane so he wouldn't have so far to walk back. And here he came, lifeless animal dangling from his hand by its long tail. The van's back latch rattled, then daylight poured inside, A.P.'s silhouette dark against the glare, slow-moving with guilt.

He gently lowered the little body onto the carpeting among the equipment. It looked like no breed of dog Delphine had ever seen. "That's not a dog," she told the air as the rear door slammed shut.

He must've heard her. "*C'est un macaque*," he said, climbing behind the wheel again, lighting a cigarette.

She watched him for a clue. "*Mais*, it's dead?"

"Probably." He checked the traffic, then drove back into its flow. "Or real close to it."

"What in the world you want with a dying *macaque*?"

It took him a while to answer. "Can't just *leave* it there, Feen…"

"Well. No."

"Can you see it from where you sit? Is it breathing?"

"I don't see blood," she said, turning back, "but it sure isn't breathing, poor little thing. What's a *macaque* doing in Louisiana? Escaped from the zoo?"

"There's some kind of facility somewhere over here on the North Shore, doing medical experiments on monkeys…"

"*Poo-yee-yi.* Got some deadly disease, and here it is next to my suitcase."

"…but this one's littler and browner than those. So it probably escaped from a car, or maybe that big truck stop. Probably some trucker's pet."

"Poor little thing. Run out of luck…"

Neither of them spoke for a while. The bright empty water of

Lake Pontchartrain stretched ahead, shoreless, as they raced onto the right-most bridge spanning its brilliance.

Delphine turned to look at him. "You want to send this little newspaper piece up to Mickey and Cam?"

"You know she won't give a shit about it." He stubbed out his cigarette. "And you think 'phenomenal' means anything at all to Cam?"

"He's seven years old, he can *read*." Delphine waved one futile hand in the air, grasping at something and failing. Because if a tree fell in a forest and nobody heard it, did that still count as a sound? If a man brought an audience to its feet but nobody he knew ever even heard about it, had it really happened? *He plays music all the time, done it since he was nine years old, but we're too used to it now to pay the slightest attention.*

She was sorry she'd spoken Mickey's name.

You were so proud to bring her home to us, boo. Leaky roof, kids fighting in the front yard, me plucking a chicken, and two-year-old Tee-Nick following the both of you in a dirty diaper I hadn't gotten around to changing yet. You changed him yourself in the houseboat, then carried him back to me—all the time laughing—so you could make out with your cheerleader in private.

We were pretty used to you and girls. All kinds of girls went crazy over good-looking boys who played in bands. But we weren't prepared for Michelle Wickham.

"He'll get in trouble I can't get him out of, messing around that rich *Texian's* daughter," Paul had worried over and over. "Boy needs to keep his *bibitte* in his pants and get his *maudit* head out of the clouds, Feen. Cameron Wickham'll squash him like a bug."

You were just too good-looking for your own good, A.P. Too smart. With such a damn hard head, couldn't nobody get through to you.

Coo Lord, look at what all happened, son.

Morning sun burnished his dark hair now. That fine, long French nose on him was Paul's, dimples Delphine's, soulful coffee-black eyes all his own. *Better-looking than ever, way more than enough to get in trouble, boo. In your late thirties now, head still hard*—tête dure.

She rode next to him like a stranger on a bus, not knowing if he was thinking about Mickey now, or how he felt about the past. Delphine didn't know what he felt about anything at all.

But the sun was shining, she wasn't in the kitchen getting Sunday dinner into the Crock Pot before Mass, and the bus ride back to Bois Sec this evening promised to be pleasurable. It was sort of nice to just be on the road for a change.

He clicked on the radio, turned up a Motown oldie, and she heard him singing along in an absent-minded way after a moment.

I'm enjoying myself, she realized. *But I hate my ponytail.*

* * *

Actually, most of what A.P. was thinking about while he smoked and drove right now was the Dead Monkey Issue. *He's no rhesus monkey, he didn't come from a lab. Somebody's pet, maybe there'll be an ad. Guess I should call 'em and tell 'em what happened.*

Yeah, and have some giant homicidal trucker coming after me with a tire iron...

"Sure is a nice day," said Feen. "I haven't been over this way in a long, long time. Any Benihanas around here anywhere?"

"Benihana...? Japanese restaurant?"

"Yeah. Went to one up in Baton Rouge last year, me and Cathy LeBlanc. The chef chops up food right in front of you like some Samurai. Talk about *good.*"

"Um... there might be one in Metairie or somewhere... don't know for sure..." *It's not like I got a whole lot of time to do something. It's going to need burying, or putting out with the garbage. But I can still make the call if there's an ad.*

"What you got against *shaving?* You got such a nice face, you ought to give the poor thing a chance sometime."

"...Talking about the monkey?"

"I'm talking about your *face.*"

Poor thing... Shaving...

"You writing some of your own songs now? That one about Mickey?"

"Um… Mostly." *Hmm. Wonder what a monkey would look like without all its hair?* "Me and Chuck Berry…"

"What kind of music you call what you're doing now?"

"No earthly idea. Ask Bee-Bee."

"Bee-Bee gets the final say on everything, I take it."

"*Mais* yeah, you saw him. Force of nature, and he gets us gigs." *Figure about ten disposable razors, maybe a bottle of cosmetic hair remover? Maybe leave a little patch around the pubic area, that'd seem more natural. Maybe some in its armpits. Stick it in the freezer.*

Her profile frowned. "He's not real friendly, is he? Only smiled at me once when you introduced us. Didn't seem surprised I was there."

"Nothing at all surprises Bee-Bee." *Except an extraterrestrial, maybe? Buy doll clothes and dress it? Planet of The Transvestite Apes?*

She looked at him closely, her made-up face suddenly twisting in glee. "What're you laughing at, you?"

He didn't know he'd laughed out loud. It made him feel guilty. "Nothing."

I killed something innocent. Doesn't matter whether it was an accident or not.

* * *

So once he got Feen to the bus station, then drove home to lift the dead animal off the van's carpet, his only option became getting a shovel out of his landlords' shed and burying it in the back yard before dark. Anything else seemed unthinkable, suddenly.

He doesn't deserve going into the garbage. A.P. examined the strange small body in awe, those tiny hands so like a human's, the feet so like hands. *I should've been paying more attention. I shouldn't've been driving so fast.*

An old T-shirt would serve as a shroud. He fetched one from inside his apartment, then hurried to get the deed done before anybody saw him. It took him a while—shovels and walking canes didn't exactly enhance each other—but he did it. Marking the grave was out of the question; he was pretty sure his landlords wouldn't be on board with this if they found out about it. *Yeah, Nelson Ryan'll scream plague-carrier even louder than Feen...*

Finally raking dead leaves over the raw place in the black dirt was the last thing he could do. Nobody would ever know what lay beneath. *Except me.*

Poor little peeshwank *had somebody who loved him. He had a name. And I killed him.*

CHAPTER FOUR

Delphine got her hair cut and permed that next week, then bought some Miss Clairol and covered her gray herself. It all came out too black, but so what. Her natural color had once been real dark.

She'd tried to tell Paul and the kids about A.P.'s revelatory performance, but Bobby and Auradele seemed uninterested in anything besides their friends and their after-school jobs—neither homework nor an older brother factored in anywhere. Paul merely spread himself out in his recliner after work, beer in hand, watching sportscasters on television and muttering, "Living on the dole, sleeping late every damn morning, I don't see where a drunk dope-fiend sets anybody a good example…"

Well.

The family tomb needed attention before *La Toussaint*. She got out there on Tuesday in the cemetery behind Our Lady of Lourdes with Cathy LeBlanc and several others in their white shrimpers' boots, plucking wall ferns from between bricks with a minimum of damage, weed-whacking and whitewashing. Purchasing pots of chrysanthemums from the florist over in Cut Off, arranging them around the names of the long-gone or newly lost.

Paul drove her out on All Saints' Eve to light a candle at the surname *Savoie*. They paused there side by side in the mild chill where a figurine of Our Lady of The Assumption and Tee-Nick's frayed teddy bear stood guard on top, but the Rosary seemed oddly inadequate now, the traditional prayers no longer covering all the bases Delphine felt needed covering.

Don't know why I'm out here, because I don't think Heaven's listening. Tee-Nick's gone wherever we all go. Years flitting by so fast...

Where's A.P.'s next gig at?

* * *

She found him down the alley and out back of his New Orleans apartment, shelling pecans with his eight fingers as the sun went down over Children's Hospital across Tchoupitoulas Street. Here she was with this glamorous new hairdo, but he made no comment about it. "Hey," was his one word.

She remembered the murk and chill of All Saints' Eve in Bois Sec. *Maybe I've brought some of it back with me.* The little roll-away bed in the kitchen was where she would sleep. She set her suitcase down next to it.

"You got to see *all* his shows?" Paul's voice was still with her. "You turning into a roadie or a groupie or what?"

"It's not his shows I'm interested in. I just got a bad feeling about him. All I see him taking is Motrin, but there's pills in his top drawer under his T-shirts. Pain meds."

"Pills going to kill him, they'd have done it long before now." Snort. Yawn.

Sometimes, Paul Savoie, I think you love acting goddam stupid more than you love any of us.

Renting the back half of one side of this shotgun double, A.P. had only one room that was neither kitchen nor bath, and that's where she went now, turning on the TV to banish all silence. The only place to watch it was from the unmade bed, where stained sheets reeked of Dior's scent *Poison* and A.P.'s own patchouli. The mental images they jointly called up were unwelcome.

The back door banged. He stood in the doorway. "Want some coffee?"

"Yeah, that sounds good. Thanks."

There were heaped ash trays everywhere. Open paperbacks. Issues of *Rolling Stone* on the floor. Stacks of stereo albums, tapes and CDs. A black guitar case rested next to his walking cane near the alley door. He returned with two mismatched cups, then sat on the edge of the mattress, popping raw pecan kernels into his mouth, flipping through a magazine while Maury Povitch held forth about paternity tests from whatever anonymous channel this was.

"You okay?" she finally had to ask over her coffee.

He shook his head.

"This isn't like you, boo, being so quiet. What's the problem?"

He drained his cup, then stood and headed for the kitchen with it, Delphine waiting for explanations, but none seemed forthcoming.

Don't push him, he's secretive. He could know for a fact that the world's going to end tomorrow and he still wouldn't tell you.

Drying his hands on a dish towel, he finally returned and began to fumble through the heaps of books and magazines and papers on the round oak table serving him as a desk, extracting a small envelope, then tossing it at her. "Look."

She caught it in mid-air. It was addressed to him in Mickey's handwriting. Even the handwriting looked blond. Delphine glanced up but he was lighting a cigarette now and staring at sparrows outside the nicotine-clouded window.

Dear Dad,

We have to write something for school about occupations. What do you do? Mom said to ask you.

It snowed last night. Mom says it is warm down there. I want to come soon. She says maybe when school is out. Terry Lanzl took me to the Jets game. He is Mom's friend. Will you take me to the super dome sometime.

Well, mom says to do homework now. I will watch T.V. later. Do you have cable? Goodbye Dad.

Your friend, Cam

No sickness, no death. Delphine was relieved. She folded her grandson's letter and stuck it back into the envelope. "*Coo!* He sure writes good-good!"

A.P. watched the sparrows. "So what do I do?"

"Sit yourself right down and answer the child's letter."

"You know what I mean. What do I *do?*—Collect goddam disability, is pretty much it."

"*Mais* you play music…"

"Don't hardly pay for the gas I spend on it." He pocketed his Zippo lighter. "When you're his age, do you even know what a father *is*, biologically speaking? Just the man who lives with your mama, could be anybody. Could be this Terry What's-His-Name, taking him to the Jets game. Y'all used to make this big deal to me, saying how St. Joseph wasn't Jesus's real father, that his real father was God and all. But Joseph was married to Mary, wasn't he? Taught little Jesus how to hammer home a nail. That made him Jesus's daddy in *my* book, all right…"

Delphine tried to call up the small blond image, big dark eyes, demanding mouth of Cam. No use. Too much time had passed. He lived too far away. There was a framed photo on her dresser back in Bois Sec, Cam at age three. It could have been of anybody's child. She wouldn't have known the difference. "But boo, he won't be seven for long. Maybe when he's older…"

"Oh yeah, yeah." A.P. nodded vigorously. "Yeah. Pull out an anatomy textbook. When him and me get down to just a letter a year: 'Dear Dad, Harvard is great. Wish you were here.'"

You need to see him more often, son. Just like I've been needing to see you.

His bad hand went up to his ear lobe, up to the gold earring. "I just wish I could say something like, 'Look, Cam—back when your mom loved me, I put a piece of myself into her. It mixed with a little piece of her, grew into a baby, and got born. That's you. We named you after our own two fathers. So you've got my eyes and you're my real son because you're made out of that piece of *me*. And I'll love you 'til I'm stone dead.' You think Mick's ever explained any of that? You think he'd understand it?"

I sure don't like that "stone dead" part. "Well, I expect he's seen enough television to have a pretty good idea about where babies come from…"

"Maybe. I don't know. He was only three when Mick finally left me for good."

Her voice was soft. "And why'd she do that?"

He shook his head, his back to her, loose black curls brushing his collar. "Because her way was the way everything had to be. Because I didn't have a way. She had the money, she was the Mom. I was nobody. I didn't know how *not* to hurt her, trying to feel like a man."

"You got some funds." She played with her wedding ring. "Buy a train ticket. Go up and see him."

"Yeah." His laugh was like a bark. "All he says is 'What'd you bring me, Dad?' And Mick bitching about my language—'Don't say bad words, don't buy him candy because he only eats organic, don't take him to see no scary movies'—and then it's all about me and her, like. This power issue. Who's got the power. I can't mean much to Cam."

"He wants you to take him to the Superdome."

His gaze came slowly over his shoulder; hit the kitchen doorway first, then hit her. With those mournful dark eyes that could outstare a dead man.

"You hungry yet?" was all she could say.

"Not really. Eating pecans all afternoon…"

" 'Cause I got a credit card and an *envie* for chicken teriyaki like you wouldn't believe."

"Lasagna in the freezer." He threw an arm at the kitchen. "Might be some pizza. Help yourself."

"Got my heart set on Benihana's, though. No Japanese places back home in Bois Sec. That's all your poor old mama wants, boo, and she's buying."

Defeated, he searched for his wallet and stuck it into a hip pocket. Undid the childproof cap from a bottle of Motrin and popped back two with Delphine's cold coffee. Reached under the bed with a toe for his footwear so that he would not have to bend. "Bee-Bee's coming by here later…"

"So how long it takes you to eat something?"

"Get heartburn when I eat too fast."

"There's Rolaids in my purse." She looked down at his feet. "Where's your socks? It's chilly out—"

"*Jesus!* Stop nagging me!" He sat on the bed, tying up his Adidas.

She understood she'd won some kind of trivial contest, but as he fetched his cane and let her out of the door into the alley, she was wishing that he'd continued to put up a fight. His passivity disturbed her.

"Feen," he said, "maybe I need a regular job."

* * *

"Mr. Bee-Bee," she approached him later that night, while A.P. was on the phone in the kitchen with the bass player, "I think you ought to know he's been talking at supper about how he should get a real job. Like your music stuff isn't one."

The man didn't even look up from his newspaper. Just grunted.

She tried again. "A.P.'s got only a high school diploma. Did offshore welding before the army, but can't now. Office jobs are out of the question. Just tempting him to Happy Hour anyway, and he's better off without *that*."

Even seated, Bee-Bee Legendre made her feel like an insect. His one good eye scanned her now with indifference. "It a free country. Man free to fail."

"*Mais* yeah, and I hate to get personal, Mr. Bee-Bee, but when you lost your eye as a child to that air rifle, was your mother there?"

His brown face was opaque.

I can't let this go. "When they took you to Charity Hospital or somewhere, did you have a mother or *mamère* or anybody coming with you, Mr. Bee-Bee?"

He didn't move, but he spoke after a moment. "Mama. My brother Lamar."

"A.P.'s my eldest. He spent time in a veterans' hospital in California, but me and my husband never got out there to see him.

And when he got transferred to the one here in New Orleans, we visited all we could. Which was hardly ever."

The single eye glittered.

"We had a five-year-old messing with some matchbooks A.P.'d collected from all the lounges he'd played at during high school, Tee-Nick just fooling around with them while nobody noticed, you'd think his little fingers would've been too small to strike any, but no. He burnt himself up. We lived at Ochsner Hospital in shifts, me and my family, while doctors tried to save him with skin grafts and operations. A.P. said don't worry about *him*, Tee-Nick's the one needing to come first. A.P. said the whole thing was *his* fault. A.P.'s fault. Leaving matches out like that when he got drafted."

Bee-Bee regarded the pale palms of his own hands lying on the newspaper in his lap like half-open roses. Delphine could hear A.P. singing part of a new composition into the telephone in the next room.

She listened. It was innate, God-given, a whiskey voice with unusual range. No choirboy's—it didn't ask permission to go wherever it wanted to go. And it followed no rules, but never hit a false note. *False* wasn't something it was. On any level.

"He'd phone me," she went on. "Trying to keep *me* going. They weren't letting him have scissors or metal tableware or anything sharp, but we didn't know that. Blaming himself for his brother's death. He swallowed floor cleaner and hand sanitizer before his bowel re-section surgery, except nobody told us. He'd had a girl he was crazy about back in high school, but her daddy pulled some strings to get him sent off to Vietnam, so now there was no one. Not even me.

"He got addicted to pain meds. Then started drinking. Just nineteen years old."

The man's shiny face gave away nothing. Its large pores were like holes that went nowhere. "He still addicted?"

"VA still prescribes 'em."

He went back to his newspaper. "Miz Savoie, it a *mean* world out there, where you been?"

CHAPTER FIVE

Sometimes I resent him, A.P. thought when he saw Bee-Bee stepping over to help him with the microphone jacks now— not like he thought A.P. couldn't bend down to get the job done, just that he himself could do it better and faster. Taking over without a word. *Acting like I'm some* couyon, *or I'm lazy. I used to do all my set-ups without anybody's help.*

He wondered how old Bee-Bee was. The man seemed like a tree. It seemed to A.P. that you could saw him in half and find rings to count.

"I ain't your sidekick," Bee-Bee had announced after their very first gig together with Lamar on keyboards, at a bar in Kenner. It had gone well, better than A.P. had been hoping for. "Call me 'partner' all you want to, Savoie—like some old cowboy movie— but I ain't. Don't expect it."

It had taken A.P. a moment to translate this. "Wait—what? '*Podna*'? Hey, that's just a word we use—I'm sorry. But, like, instead of 'man' or 'dude'? Where I'm from? I'm sorry... I don't mean anything demeaning by it... I'll try to stop saying it..."

The darker one scowled and shook his head, unsatisfied. "White character's always the star. Black man's just his sidekick."

"*The Cosby Show,*" A.P. couldn't help mentioning the exception.

"Bullshit. White man's sidekick's always a wise, saintly black brother like no real man ever lived. No balls. Only white men get to have a pair. Well, I *got* balls—older and bigger than yours, Savoie. Don't fuck with me."

Whoa. "I'll try not to."

"I ain't no saint and I ain't your sidekick. You're mine. Remember that. Stay humble."

As if I know how to be a rock star.

It had once been just him and his guitar re-strung upside down so he could fret with his good hand, A.P. doing invisible backup studio work in New York City where Mickey labored on getting her Ph.D. from NYU. During the rise of punk rock, it'd seemed the acme of *punk* to several bands to actually have him onstage—one of them insisting he cover his bad hand with stage blood first, which he did. It made the pick kind of hard to hold, but still. He didn't care, when he was drunk. The band didn't care either. They, too, were drunk. But Mickey hadn't approved, on any level. She said it was humiliating.

When I just wanted to come home and make love to you, Mick. The only way I could shut your mouth was to kiss it.

Mickey said he drank too much. Mickey said he stayed out too late. Mickey said he hung out with low-lifes. Mickey said he was smart enough to get a better job. Mickey said and said.

Kiss you to shut you up. Either that, or just leave.

Sometimes he had performed solo in bars where they'd never had live music before and let him work because he asked for no more than free drinks and tips. *Always a couch I could crash on. Always a girl I could stay with.*

But one night in New Orleans, after Mickey finally said "Never come back" and he'd gone home to Louisiana and was doing old Tom Petty material, this one-eyed black man sauntered up after the last song to say "Stop trying to sound like Tom Petty. You ain't Tom Petty. You don't remind me of Tom Petty. You don't remind me of *anybody*, as a matter of fact, that Coonass accent and bad legs. Name's Walter 'Bee-Bee' Legendre, and I might can make you some real green money, if you get out your own way."

Always acting like it's some kind of contest between us, A.P. thought now, standing upright, displaced by Bee-Bee's bulk. Relinquishing the cords, yet grateful for the help. He retreated into the men's room. *I'd thank him if I thought he was doing it for me.*

He could hear the sound checks going on out front, Lamar's keyboards, Kyle's bass. *Blang blang blang* went his own guitar—he knew its voice the way a father knows his child's.

"Daddy? Daddy?" He heard Cam in his mind, saw his small solemn face in the doorway of the bedroom where A.P. sat smoking in the Manhattan dark, bottle on the floor by his foot. "Mommy's locked herself in the bathroom, Daddy. She's crying and won't come out."

Cam. *Jesus.* Wrong train of thought before a show.

He only glanced at the mirror; he knew what he looked like. Patrons paid him little attention as they came and went, used the urinals, washed and dried their hands. His arms were impressively muscled, shoulders and upper body sculpted—courtesy of dragging the rest of him around—but he moved with little grace. *Even so, there's always women waiting for me to come through any door. Pretty girls flashing me from down front, all kinds of women backstage. Like, maybe with intuition telling 'em a walking cane ain't the only big stick I got...*

Leaning against a sink, going over the lyrics of *Anna Banana* in a whisper, he tried to regress. Young A.P. Savoie with a Beatle haircut, driving around all night with the Beach Boys on the radio. How it had been to have great moves. To run. To run with a football mashed against his ribs. To perform onstage with his uncle's band, bouncing in the light and the joy. To hold Mickey Wickham closer than close, so she could feel how hard she made him.

Feen reached up to adjust the collar of his flannel shirt when he came out into the corridor. No getting away from her for long. "I look all right?" he asked.

"Like you been cutting sugar cane for a week..."

"Got any Motrin on you?" He put a hand to his back. "I got this... little..." But it was a big ache, and it said *Daddy, Mommy's locked herself in the bathroom*—

Lamar and Kyle were already out front, adjusting equipment,

with Bee-Bee at his sound board. But A.P. reached back into his hip pocket with two fingers to fish out his wallet. Flipping hurriedly through the plastic windows, glare glinting off the surfaces, he found the photo.

Cam. Make Daddy break a leg, son. Don't let Daddy forget the lyrics.

Nobody was looking in his direction when he put the photograph of his little boy to his lips for a second, tasting the warmth of his own body heat. Then he stuffed the wallet back into his pocket and went onstage.

* * *

Dear Cam,

Remember me? I'm your mamere Delphine Savoie. Your father was my little boy as you know. He put a peace of himself into your mom which is a baby and is you. That is what a father is. So you will always have only one real father and he loves you.

He plays music. I am putting a news paper picture in here. That is him on the left with his head turn. I know it is him because I was there.

Hey Cam. I am also sending you a check. Let your mom put you on a plane for Christmas and we can see the super dome. Don't tell your father, it is a surprise. Write me at my own address in Bois Sec and tell me the flight. I will be right there to meet you.

"I'd like to dedicate this next number to the people back home in Bois Sec, Louisiana," A.P.'s amplified voice came echoing from out front, and Delphine put her pen down. "Y'all know Bois Sec? No? It's way down the bayou between a shrimp-packing plant and a shipyard, and stereotypically we like to hunt, eat, dance, and fight. And *faire l'amour*, of course, which the girl in this song raised to a fine art when I was in high school. –And I do mean *raised*."

Loud boozy guffaws. It was Saturday night in Biloxi, they were ready to laugh at fire extinguishers.

Delphine heard him pick the first few notes of *Anna Banana,* another one of these new songs he was writing, a good upbeat account of a very bad girl. It was rapidly becoming a favorite of Delphine's because Mickey wasn't in it.

> I got to go now Cam. But here is some French for you.
> I can not spell that either but here goes. Je tam mo tee.
> That means I love you my little boy. Give your mom my
> fondest hello.
> Your mamere, Delphine

She ran outside and dropped the letter into a mailbox a block and a half away. The Gulf surged at high tide across the dim white sand on the other side of the highway, the night smelling like salt and old love. Biloxi was stars and black palm trees at the beach edge of the city. She wanted to go home.

Delphine resented A.P. suddenly, this apprehension he was causing her. He'd been such a low-maintenance child. It was unfair for him to cause her so much grief now, so late in the game. She wished for a moment that he was back in New York, still Mickey's problem.

She patted the mailbox before trotting back to the club, urging it to bring her some kind of relief.

CHAPTER SIX

A telephone rang in the night.

He swam up out of a dream about sharks on bicycles and got one hand on the receiver before the answering machine could kick in. Somebody had died. Pop had had a stroke. Cam had fallen down a manhole. A.P. put it to his earring. "Yeah?"

"You manipulative asshole!" came Mickey's very awake voice, sharp as an ice pick. "What're you doing?"

Something coughed into the other pillow. He reached out and encountered soft female anatomy. "Nothing, at the moment…"

"*You* put her up to this, didn't you?" Mick's voice was rich with that I'll-claw-your-hide-off rage he knew so well. "I just hope you're both satisfied, pal! Cam is whining and pitching a fucking *fit*, he's locked himself in his room and won't—!"

"Wait a minute, wait a minute—" He hiked himself up onto one elbow, trying to consult his watch in near total darkness. "What's the matter with Cam? He sick?"

" 'Sick', my ass! He's pitching a goddam *fit*, that's what he's doing! How *could* you, Adrien? Don't you think I've got enough problems with him?"

"Babe, I'm sorry. I'm sorry, babe."—Used to apologizing for stuff he never remembered doing, he meant it.

"We live hundreds of miles away! There're child molesters on airplanes!"

...Mais *yeah, no doubt there are. You've probably got the statistics at your fingertips.* "I'm sorry, babe," he had to say again after a moment, sober but helpless. "I'm not following you..."

"*Delphine*! Delphine's letter! Cam's been *impossible*, waving it around, secretly trying to call Delta Airlines—!"

He collapsed back into the musky pillows with an instantaneous headache: *Feen.*

The body beside him rolled over in the dark and snuggled its head under his chin, mumbling "What time is it, baby? I got to get up, I'm on the early shift..."

"Who's that?" Mick had excellent hearing. "Who's with you?"

"Houseguest. Christine Reo."

"It's *Kirsten*," the girl under his chin corrected him.

"Well," said Mickey, "if you think for one second I'm going to let Cam come down there and be exposed to your exemplary life style, you've got another think coming!" Her Texas sure came out whenever she was pissed. "So just take that blank check and stick it somewhere *real* private, and stop the hell contacting me."

" 'Blank check'," he repeated. "No idea what you're talking about."

"*God*, I hate it when you're drunk and stupid."

"I'm *couyon*, yes," he agreed cautiously. "Drunk, no."

"*God*, you don't have the least idea of what I'm talking about, do you." It was not a question. He could hear her defeat. "Look, Adrien. Delphine sent Cam a peculiar letter concerning... well... fatherhood. It arrived yesterday, and he got to it before I could screen it. Asking him to come down there for Christmas. She even enclosed a blank check for the airfare."

"Aw *Jesus*..."

"I told him no, I said wait until the summertime, I said it doesn't suit Mom to go yet—he's *impossible*. He's told every kid in the third grade he's going down to New Orleans to hunt alligators. Yelling, slamming doors... Terry says to just wait it out—"

"Terry Lanzl."

"Yes. Good friend of ours.—He says to just wait it out, and I wish I knew what Cam's therapist would say, but I can't reach her…"

Kirsten clicked on the bedside lamp, beginning to dress herself, A.P.'s lust rekindling as he watched her fastening her bra. *Christ,* he thought, *we both got lucky last night. She's a hot redhead, and I'm not a serial killer.* "Mick—babe—I didn't know about Feen. But I'm sorry. I'll straighten it out. You know I'd never do anything to get Cam all worked up. You know that."

"The woman is a *case!* She's got him all hot to go now, and I can't say that I can't afford it, and I can't tell him to wait until school's out, because school *will* be out for the holidays…!"

Feen. She made me clean fish with a knife when I was six. She let me take out the boat alone. Let me smoke at twelve. Now she won't even let me wipe my own ass.

"Look look look," he said into the phone, weary. The sky was still black outside. He put a forearm over his eyes to keep the lamp light out. "Why don't we just let him come?"

—But hell, talk about your wrong approaches, letting yourself in for another lecture about what an unfit parent and irresponsible jack-ass you are…

Yet Mickey did not lecture. A.P. could hear her breathing.

He sat up, hungry now, hunger born of remote possibility burning in his stomach like last night's pizza. *Don't be getting your hopes up, she's just clearing her throat so she can tell you what a flake your mama is in case you didn't hear her the first time.* "Mickey?"

"Just let me think for a second, okay?"

"But you can come too, babe, see? Bring along your friend Terry, if you want. Bring your mama. Stay at a hotel, you'll never even have to see me. Y'all can have Christmas together—I won't butt in, I swear. Just let me have Cam for a day. Just one day. Then y'all can fly back, and he can tell his friends about how he saw mermaids in the bayou or whatever, and everybody can calm down. I'll sing for him right here, and I won't do nothing rougher than Barry Manilow, I swear—Mickey?"

"Lord, won't you let a person *think?*"

"Hey, I don't need your answer *now.*" He was scared of pushing her into a premature no. "You just look at it from all angles, then let me know what you want to do. Talk it over with Terry." *Who's probably showering in your bathroom right now. Like I'm entitled to any objections.*

Kirsten was waving goodbye to him from the doorway, clearly unhappy.

"Wait," he mouthed at her. "*Please* wait, I'll drive you home, honey…"

But she shook her head and left, hopeless and abrupt. He did understand why.

"—if it's okay with you, Adrien," Mickey was going on when he listlessly put the receiver back to his ear, "maybe Terry'll come with us, that's not a bad idea. I mean, it's about time we got over being uncomfortable in each other's company, you and I. For Cam's sake. You know?"

He had to take a few deep steadying breaths before he spoke. "Yeah."

"You're the father of my child, so it's not like I can put you in the rear view mirror for good, not while he's a minor, anyway—I'm working through all that stuff in therapy now."

Don't tell me I was just your mistake, Mick. It might be true, but don't say it.

"We used to be friends, you and I," she said. "Maybe we ought to try it again. The way you made me laugh. I miss that, pal."

I don't believe it. I'm deader than the monkey for you. Whatever mistake we used to enjoy making between us, it's deader than the monkey. "Well, go on back to bed—"

"Some of us *work* in the mornings! I have a class of undergrads at ten!"

"—and don't get nuts. It'll all work out." *Here's where we used to say "I love you" to each other. Here's where we just say "Good-bye", these days.*

Lord, I hope she don't bring her mama.

* * *

Mickey hung up the phone with shaking hands, breakfast almost ready. She'd have to wake Cam for school in a minute, as soon as his oatmeal was done. Stirring it with a wooden spoon like this steadied her. *I didn't see that coming. Me telling Adrien "Yes".*

Cam needed waking. In a minute.

But I never saw him coming in the first place…

Daddy and me, going fishing on a Saturday right after relocating to Louisiana, the boat behind us on its trailer. Real hot day—July—and we're in the store at the marina buying cold drinks. A tanned shirtless boy in denim cut-offs rings us up, asking if we also need any "bett".

"Bett?" We don't get it.

"Bett. Bett." He tries with his hands to make us see. "What fish eat? What you put on your hooks? Y'all must be from Texas."—such artless amusement. Is he psychic? Never seen dimples in the tops of somebody's cheeks before, and I can't stop looking. Hair black as a Choctaw's, smooth skin glossed with sweat, face and body of a Greek statue, wildly beautiful…

Cam. In a minute…

Our license plates say Texas, but still. My God. Magic! A narrow river of downy dark hair runs from his navel into his cut-offs, and my knees turn to jelly.

In a minute…

Long, strong fingers scribble something on a store receipt—all in capital letters—and tuck it into my hand when Daddy isn't looking: I'M GOING TO MARRY YOU. The place in my palm where he touches me is hot, and I don't think it's ever cooled off since.

The sound of his voice can still make my hands shake. I probably still turn pink—no way to hide it.

Jesus, I sure hope Terry can't go.

CHAPTER SEVEN

"But why're you so sore at me, you?" Delphine, fresh off the bus from Bois Sec that next Friday morning, couldn't understand it. "You're getting to see Cam, yes? That's good, isn't it?"

"Figure it out for yourself." He did up his good shirt, nearly tearing two buttons off. "You're so brilliant, *you* figure it out."

"Lord, you're the worst-tempered person sometimes! No wonder Mickey couldn't get along with you!"

He leveled a finger at her. "I'm not tolerating any more interference, you understand me?"

She stood there, palms up. "But what did I *do?*"

"Forget it. Just forget it. Hand me my watch, please. It's there on the dresser."

She looked at him while he tucked in his shirt tail. He'd shaved off his beard. She'd almost forgotten what his face looked like. "Where in the world're you going?"

Tying up his Adidas, he muttered, "Doesn't concern you."

She sat on his bed. "I'm sorry, boo…"

Mute, he pulled a comb through his hair. Knotted a wide flowered thrift-shop silk tie at his collar, then got into a vintage suit jacket with padded shoulders. Delphine sat motionless as he reached for keys where they lay among the litter on the table top.

He met her eyes, firm nude lip set, jaws clenched, looking healthy and not to be trifled with. Startlingly handsome. But then his expression softened a little and he bent to give her a quick hug. "It's okay, let's just forget it. See you later at rehearsal."

She said nothing. Reached for his hand, finally. But it and his silver-headed cane were already out the door.

* * *

A.P. and Bee-Bee were at the kitchen table, elbows on it, smoking and arguing, when she got to Bee-Bee's later that evening with snacks and cold drinks from the Time Saver. Neither glanced up at her advent. Bee-Bee's wife said nothing, only nodded.

"...got them plastic heads, that's why I don't want no rock drummer," Bee-Bee was saying, voice low, mouth not a foot away from A.P.'s earring. "Don't vibrate enough. Whereas Laskey's got them Slingerlands, all wood shells. Got a regular head on 'em."

A.P. finally noticed Delphine and gave her a wave, as she opened the fridge to stash away the soft drinks. "But how we going to pay Laskey, Beeb? He'll want rehearsal pay. I'll have more income now, but it's not going to let me give him what he's used to."

"Income?" Delphine's ears rotated like a cat's.

"Yeah, Beeb and I talked it over," A.P. popped the top off the can of cola Delphine handed him. "I think I can kind of keep this band on retainer, if I can give them rehearsal pay. Can't afford no blue-chip percussion, though..."

She regarded the man's eyepatch, not at all happy. "Mr. Bee-Bee ain't getting enough money to suit him? You got to give him a raise?"

"I ain't getting rehearsal pay, Miz Savoie." The deep voice was patient. "Longshoreman making good money, I help pay the band out my own pocket same as your boy here."

A.P. lay a palm on the table. "Feen, you remember a hit record, back in—like—1975 or something? Song called *Don't Tell Me*, recorded right here in New Orleans and went national?"

"No."

"That was Lamar Legendre, Bee-Bee's brother. Bee-Bee produced it. They know what they're doing. Some big gigs coming up, too."

"Potential national exposure," Bee-Bee added. "National press."

"You mentioned 'more income'."

"Got myself a job this morning. Maggio's Records and Tapes, starting the Monday after Thanksgiving. I ain't no manager there or nothing, just going to sell stuff. But at least Cam'll see me get up in the mornings and go—"

"I'm calling Laskey, yes or no?" Bee-Bee interrupted.

If Bee-Bee Legendre's as good as A.P. says, why's he a longshoreman and not a rich record producer? Delphine got up to use the bathroom, first turning on the water in the lavatory so that the men in the kitchen wouldn't hear her tinkle. These old shotgun houses had all their plumbing placed right together.

And I don't even know why I'm here. Nobody cares if I go or stay.

Probably not even Paul. Paul's not missing me. It's football season.

Her eyes filled with sloppy emotion. She smeared her mascara with one abrupt hand as she wiped at her face.

"Feen?" A.P. called from the kitchen, merry. "You fall in?"

They were smoking dope and into the Doritos when she took her seat at the table again, A.P. and Bee-Bee now joined by Lamar and Kyle, all passing a joint. Bee-Bee's wife came and went. Nothing was getting rehearsed.

He'll lose his disability.

A.P., exhilarated, was telling everybody all about the Christmas gifts he planned to buy for his son, computer stuff and football equipment and games with Japanese names that Delphine had never heard of. He took out his photo of Cam and passed it around like the joint, reaching finally for her hand in stoned reconciliation. She sat there rubbing the stumps of his missing fingers while she heard him running on.

Lord, can there be any gadget under the sun, any kind of toy or game that Michelle Wickham and her boy friend haven't bought for Cam already?

Her dream that night was beyond ghastly, A.P. lying broken on a floor and bleeding. The only person standing over him was Tee-Nick.

CHAPTER EIGHT

The Savoie house in Bois Sec had people everywhere in it for Thanksgiving.

Looking not even remotely like a show place, or anything tourists would want to photograph, still it exerted a powerful hold over those who'd grown up under its roof.

Fronting the water a mile down Bayou Bois Sec from where that waterway branched off from Bayou Lafourche at the marina, built on a narrow lot by Paul's grandfather beyond the town's original limits, it existed in a constant state of de-renovation. They'd painted it a number of times but now the orangey-yellow of cypress was showing through peeling white again, the windows leaking in heavy rains. Extra rooms added onto it as needed had unbalanced its formerly-symmetrical, traditional floor plan, and its drinking water had once come from the large cistern, still on bricks out back —used these days to water vegetables in the garden back there. A plaster statue of Our Lady of The Assumption out front in Delphine's irises spread her hands over the spot where A.P. had once helped Tee-Nick bury a dead puppy, and that was pretty much it.

Never going to appear in House Beautiful, Delphine shook her head.

She stood in the damp yard now, arms folded, looking at

nothing. Afternoon sun came hazy through hanging Spanish moss and the branches of oaks. Children chased each other in and out of the shed in back and onto the dock in front, their dads leaning against the fenders of vehicles and talking, and she finally put one shoe in front of the other and started back toward the house, autumn's last mosquitos humming around her ankles and trying to get at her through her jeans.

A.P. hadn't come home with her. He said he'd be playing four nights in the French Quarter, backing up somebody else.

She paused now at the screen door in back and wiped her feet. Black-bellied whistling ducks carried on like maniacs across the water.

"Sometimes I think I'm the only one in this family's got good sense, me," she told Auradele as she came into the kitchen, her observation pitched loud enough where Paul could hear it in the next room. "Some people value being ignorant."

Fourteen-year-old Aura didn't look up from her apple-dicing. Lolo and Bay-Bay, busy with mirlitons and oysters, never turned around. They knew their mother's remarks weren't meant for them.

Paul knew who they were meant for. Delphine raised her face and there he was, beer in hand, leaning against the door jamb, eyes narrowed so that the crow's-feet spread well into his temples. "Ignorance is *bliss,* Feen. And you sure could use a little, babe…"

She took out flour for the roux, banging the skillet down on the stove. "You never even asked about him."

"Lot of stuff I don't ask about. Didn't ask you about the Dow Jones, either."

"Go watch your *maudit* game. Damn Steelers might get in the end zone while you waste your time in here."

Daughters and daughters-in-law gossiped out on the *galerie,* babies in their laps, while sons and sons-in-law monitored football in the living room. Grandchildren whooped from all directions. Delphine silently browned her roux as Paul watched. "Okay," he gave in, finally, "let's start over: How's he doing?"

"Not bad. Opening a few eyes, music-wise. And Mickey and little Cam's coming for Christmas."

The way his brows went up brought her some satisfaction, but "Stuck-up *cocotte*" was all he muttered. Then he turned around, soles squeaking on the linoleum, and Delphine heard the plop when he sprawled into his recliner in the next room.

"You know why he didn't come home for Thanksgiving?" she shouted at him over the sportscaster. "It's that mouth on you! *That's* why!"

The invisible recliner made no response.

She motioned to Bay-Bay to take over for her at the stove top and stomped into the living room. Hefty sons-in-law moved over on the sofa to make room for her, not meeting her eyes. Slim little Bobby glanced up, pulling at the sparse teenage moustache he was trying to grow, then sighed and hitched up his jeans and slouched past his mother without a word. Because Delphine wasn't going away. She stood there planted, oven mitt in hand, until the others got heavily to their feet and lumbered out into the kitchen for more beer.

A window and the TV lit Paul where he sat smoking.

Her arms flopped to her sides. "We got all seven of our living children here with us this afternoon, Paul, all but one. Because—"

"*En Français.*" He nodded meaningfully towards the kitchen. Most of this younger generation had been raised with television and spoke only English.

She sighed. Then came all the way inside the room and perched on the arm of the recliner, making it return to upright. Crooking a perspiry arm around his neck, she brushed her fingers up into the gray hair above his ear. He reached over her thighs for his Bic, lighting another smoke. "Look," she began in soft French, "I know it's hard on you to have me gone so much of the time lately…"

"Harder on Bobby and Aura. Worrying that we might be splitting up, you and me. You with that new hairdo. Got a new man?"

"Just you. Always."

"I know that. They don't."

"So maybe I need to take them with me next time. To see A.P. onstage. Make them proud of him, I bet. It's not like he's still way up in New York City. We're only ninety miles from New Orleans, Bobby could drive—"

"When was the last time A.P. hauled his ass down here to see *them*?"

She made a popping sound with her mouth, then started to stand. He held her wrist. "Listen, Feen. When I was his age, I had me a wife I did right by. Kids I did right by. Five days a week—more—I got up early, hauled my ass to the shipyard, and did my job. Still do. None of you living like royalty, but we didn't starve then and we're not starving now."

"How many *crippled* men you work with?"

"You're never here—I could be working with rodeo clowns or beauty queens, for all you know. And coddling A.P. like you do, that's not helping him, Feen. We love him. You love him, I love him. But you can't keep treating him like some child."

"All I know is," said Delphine, "I got this bad feeling. Like he's headed for disaster."

"Mickey Wickham's the damn disaster—*cocotte maudite*—always making him want stuff he doesn't get. *College*."

She shook her head, remembering A.P. in his high school days reading books Mickey gave him out there in the dry-docked houseboat he slept in. The teacher in his grade school before that, saying "Mrs. Savoie, we think your son is gifted." The news had made her so proud, so happy. This boy could go *anywhere*.

"College might've kept him out the army, Paul," she said now. "Tack welding didn't."

"My brother's band sure as hell wasn't going to."

"Okay—congratulations!—you're a two-fisted man, but he's only got a fist-and-a-half. He brought us together when he was born, you and me. *Please* don't let him come between us now."

"You sprung him on me out of the blue, Feen. I wasn't even sure he was mine."

"But you married me anyway."

"Because my father said it was the right thing to do. Babe, I was somebody who *respected* my father. I listened to my father. Unlike someone I could mention."

"Paul…"

"You see A.P. listening to even *one* thing I say? Ever? I told him, 'Don't mess around a rich man's daughter, son.' I said, 'Good welders make more money than many college graduates.' I said, 'Shipyard'll give you better job security than offshore, A.P.' I told him until I was blue in the face, 'Playing music's no real kind of career.' And I said, 'Don't trust Cameron Wickham.' —Might as well have been talking to myself. And everything went to hell. Everything went right straight into hell."

"You sorry you married me?"

"No." He took her hand. "I'm sorry about a lot of things, but that's not one of them."

Her voice got wobbly. "We'll never get over Tee-Nick until A.P. gets over it, Paul. And he *can't*. Every year goes by, I think: 'Well, maybe he's finally forgiving himself. Maybe this is the time.' But I never see it happening."

"It wasn't his fault, what happened to Tee-Nick. Nobody else blames him, Feen."

"Yes, we do," she spoke the truth. "In our heart of hearts, Paul. Both of us."

He suddenly pushed her aside, scrambled to his feet, and strode rapidly to the bathroom, slamming the door. But Delphine had caught a glimpse of reddening eyes.

She stood, finally. Stiffly. Going back into the kitchen, taking the turkey from the oven. Bay and Lolo helped pour off the juices and save them. Nobody spoke.

Paul eventually reappeared for another beer, his face informing Delphine the subject was closed. She threw the roasting pan into the stained sink and ran water into it.

"We all *do* love him, Mama," Bay-Bay ventured after a while. "A.P., I mean. We just don't know him anymore."

"Somebody's invented the telephone," Delphine said, "last time I heard."

A squall came from outside, a child pleading, "Tiffany *hit* me! Tiffany's *hitting* me!"

"Lord." Bay threw down her potholder. "That's Jason, he's such a little pansy. Let me go separate 'em..."

So when can you finally lock them out of your life, your kids? Delphine wondered, almost too numb to breathe. *How old do they have to be before you can finally say Goodbye and good luck—and I'll love you forever—but don't come back because you're killing me?*

* * *

He was working on a song that Thanksgiving night, absorbed in a tricky measure until loud pounding and a shout came through the thin wall: "Savoie! You play that goddam song one more time, I'm going to come over and put your lights out!" Okay. So his landlords were home.

"Sorry!" he yelled at the plasterboard, thwarted. Fuming at the wall for a moment, but then put down the guitar. *They've got a point.*

A lopsided wire Christmas tree stood naked at his window. It hadn't been lopsided when he bought it at Schwegmann's the evening before, but an amp had fallen on it during the ride home. He left it as it was, empathizing. *Bee-Bee'd say to it 'Stay humble.'*

So what's the best way to put lights on a tree? He couldn't recall how Mickey had done it, or Feen. It seemed a good idea now to just start at the top with one end of the light string, and just spiral on down. He spiraled. Two of the bulbs did not light up when he plugged it in.

He clicked on the battered portable TV nearby and found football. Didn't matter who was playing.

On with the ornaments...

The words of his song kept coming. He heard the melody in his mind trying to catch each word, get under each one just right with just the right note, like a wide receiver out for a pass. *Don't need the guitar, I can sing it. Quiet-quiet.* Satisfied, he tried out phrase after phrase on his distorted bulbous reflections in the glass ornaments, all nose.

When standing made him uncomfortable, he sat on the bed and watched the lights shine for a while. They were just cheap little bulbs, ordinary, but if you watched them blink off and on long enough, they became beautiful. He lit a cigarette.

Like Heaven. I remember.

Maybe it hadn't been literal Heaven, but he had floated up like helium on February 22, 1969, courtesy of Viet Cong artillery. To blazing white light, so strong it broke up into colors in his peripheral vision. *I didn't want to come back down.*

The telephone rang. He ignored it. Answer machine would pick up, if it was on.

It wasn't.

I saw so many bad things in Nam. So many. I helped cause some of 'em. But the very worst thing I saw in those days was with my mind, not my eyes: Tee-Nick on fire.

He finally stood and went to the table to look at a calendar. *I still see it. When I can't sleep.*

The date of Cam's arrival was circled, the flight number penciled in. A.P. counted all the days between then and now. He counted them twice.

I need a happy thing, me.

The phone rang again.

"Yeah?" he said into the receiver.

"You interested in opening for Frieda Washington's come-back tour at Tipitina's?" came Bee-Bee's deep voice.

Frieda Washington—she still alive? She used to be big-big. On, like, American Bandstand. *Lot of hits, but that was years ago.*

A.P. was wary. "You shitting me, *podna?*"

"We got December twenty-first and twenty-second. Two sets each night. Good press coverage. Somebody coming who might be interested in fronting the money for an album."

A.P. lay back on the pillows, noticing what a solid ceiling he had on his way down. His voice detached from the rest of him. "Mickey and Cam'll be here then..."

"That a problem?"

Is this my happy thing? Coming right when I need it? "Hell no!" he rubbed a hand over his face and mouth in astonishment, ambushed by his own sudden joy. "Fuck, Beeb, you're *magic!* You're Superman!"

"We cut an album, we're going to need more material. Got that new song written yet?"

"Yes," he lied.

"Happy Thanksgiving." And Bee-Bee hung up without another word.

A.P. sat up, feet cold, but he didn't want to bend down in a shoe search. He padded barefoot into the kitchen, opening the refrigerator's freezing compartment, unable to stop smiling. His face hurt from it. He reached inside, under the frozen lasagna, and took out celebratory Thanksgiving marijuana. *Need to get rid of this before Cam comes, but he ain't here yet.*

Another happy thing to be thankful for.

CHAPTER NINE

They didn't seem to want him to really do anything at Maggio's Records and Tapes on his first day, except price new stock and learn to use the computerized cash register. No one that he knew came in. He was given thirty minutes for lunch.

Every time he looked up, Mike Maggio was studying him from the counter where tickets for upcoming concerts were sold. *I got something stuck in my teeth? Pigeon shat on me somewhere?*

He rang up a classical CD and handed the customer her change. *Ink on my face?*

"Hey, A.P.?" Mike came on over to the register, pulling up his khakis where his belly forced them down. "I heard you mentioning Gershwin to that customer. You like Gershwin?"

"Well, *Rhapsody In Blue*, most definitely... *Porgy and Bess*... *Concerto in F* does nothing for me, though."

"You got classical training, or what?"

A.P. logged up the title of the CD he had just sold. "No. Learned from my grandfather. Who played, like, five or six different instruments but couldn't read a note. Neither can I."

"Let me ask you something personal—and I hope you don't mind—but how you play so well with that bum hand?"

"Use a heavy pick with a high-friction coating." The question didn't bother him like it would have when he was younger and tried to keep his hand artfully hidden. He showed it to Maggio, the stumps of his missing ring finger and pinky. "Took me a while to get the hang of it, I used to think I'd never learn to play left-handed. But I do okay now, actually."

"Yeah, I know. Saw you at the Maple Leaf a few weeks ago. You're better than 'okay', you know that?"

Yes, thought A.P. with a brief rise of honest pride. He smiled.

Mike reached over and awkwardly pounded him on the shoulder, then waved affably and went back to the ticket counter to whisper to his wife. *Jesus,* A.P. realized with dumbfounded pleasure, *my boss is a fan.*

It was just before closing time when—*shit, no!*— Feen popped unexpectedly through the glass doors, dyed hair frizzed to within an inch of its life, designer jeans so tight he could make out her underwear line beneath. Now he would have to spend his brief time before rehearsal with accounts of who's married and who's dropped dead in Bois Sec, and How The Family Spent Thanks-giving, instead of the brief nap he'd promised himself.

"I was going to bring you some mirliton dressing," she came over to the cash register, looking all around at the Madonna and Bob Dylan and Bruce Springsteen posters on the wall, "but that fat *bioque* Bay's married to ate it all."

Mike and Carla Maggio were sure watching from their station at the tall ticket counter. *Hell, I'm tired,* thought A.P., pulling on his jacket and waving the two of them goodbye. *I'll introduce everybody some other time. She's only sixteen years older than me, I hope they're not thinking girl friend…*

He took her arm, and she bore up under his weight as if she thought he was leaning on her. Annoyed suddenly, he slipped his hand under her elbow and propelled her ruthlessly out of the door and into the street.

"I left my stuff at your apartment already," she said, as he let her into the van.

He threw his cane in. Climbed up to the driver's seat, then backed out into traffic.

"I got you some socks on sale." Her voice was uncertain.

"…Thanks." He took out his Zippo and lit a smoke at the first red light on Magazine Street. *What's it to you, if your mama needs to baby you? Can't you indulge the woman? What's the matter, your manhood so shaky and so tenuous that tiny little Feen here can blow it away? She's got nothing better to do. Kids just about all grown and gone…*

Neon lights came and went over her face in his peripheral vision. *She was once much taller than me.* He remembered her slim strength, lugging the younger children up the wooden steps where he lay underneath out of the sun on hot days, reading his comic books. Her singing. Everybody on her side of the family, they were just born musical.

I remember. She sang me my first lyric: "Dans les bons heureux temps…"

"In the good old days"—went its words—*"petticoats lasted for a hundred years." It was a girl's song, and she was still a girl. So what could it mean to me?*

—Besides the fact that girls also mourn the Good Old Days?

* * *

"Hey, Feen?" A.P. had his arms full of dirty sheets as he passed the door. "Somebody knocking—can you get it for me, please?"

He heard the latch click behind him. Threw the sheets into the hamper in the bathroom and was coming to join her, but she shut it again and turned the key. "Nobody there, boo."

But I heard something. He unlocked the door and stuck his head out.

A wet gleam on the stoop caught a streetlight.

He crouched awkwardly and reached a finger into it. A trail of dark splashes went down his steps and down the alley to the street. Reddening his fingertip… He put it to his nose, already knowing.

Footprints in it.

Loud voices suddenly came through the far wall, from the landlords' half of the house. A.P. slammed the door, then lurched to the wallboard to pound on it with the flat of his hand. "Mr. Ryan? Hey, Mr. Ryan? Y'all okay over there?"

No answer.

Feen was watching him as he limped around her to the closet for the 9mm Ruger on the top shelf. "Boo? What in the world…?"

"I don't know yet." He pushed her against the bed, then up onto it. "Stay right here. Don't move."

She froze. He had used his infantry corporal's voice.

Shoving his weapon under his belt, he hustled himself outside with his cane, seeing nothing at the alley's end but the cool quiet of the streetlight and a glimpse of traffic passing. Small alarming puddles continued past the alley gate and on up the sidewalk, the print of a sneaker sole distorting some of them. Every alarm bell in his gut rang *emergency*. Running was something he couldn't manage, but he could hop/skip/jump on his right leg pretty fast if he had to.

The splotches stopped on the Ryans' front stoop.

Hauling himself up its steps by the railing—*Shit, somebody's murdered somebody?*— He saw light through the opaque shade in the door's windowed center. Heard argumentative voices, one of them female.

He raised his bad hand and knocked.

Then took the safety off his handgun. He'd filed it down years ago to a hair trigger, responsive to the merest touch. *Might be my post-traumatic stress disorder, but don't emergencies require speed?*

Yet it was only his landlord who opened the door, as normal as tap water in a greasy undershirt, yawning. Some televised detective show blared behind him. But there was blood on the floor. A.P. looked past the man to where Mrs. Ryan was kneeling near the TV to wipe at it. "Y'all… ahh… having a problem?"

Mrs. Ryan glanced up. "Hey, dawlin'."

"Oh! Wow! Sorry!" Here came a young man in splotched LSU athletic shorts, a fresh roll of Bounty in one hand, bloody towel pressed to his matted hair with the other. "You the guy from next door, right? Look, I'm sorry—I had the wrong side of the house."

"My nephew." Ryan jerked his head. "Kevin."

"Training for the marathon—I was in the park up the street," Kevin handed his aunt the roll of paper towels, then stood there bare-chested, embarrassed, head tilted and one eye blinking at A.P. from under the makeshift bandage. "And I, like, ran under this tree limb or something in the dark. I'm from out of town... Got my directions all screwed, maybe I'm concussed...?"

A.P. stepped inside with his cane, put the safety back on the Ruger, then moved the kid's hand and the towel out of the way.

"I'm sorry, man." Kevin looked pitiful.

" 'S'okay," said A.P. "Just let me see." *Blood never stays under the skin where it belongs, does it?*

"He need stitches?" asked Mrs. Ryan. "I can't stand to look."

A fold of scalp hung loose at the hairline. A.P. pressed the towel back into place. "Wouldn't hurt. And there's the concussion issue..."

"You going to drive him, Nelson?" the woman asked her husband.

"Ain't dressed. You do it."

"I'm sorry," Kevin apologized to nobody in particular. Appearing befuddled and concerned.

"I'll drive him," A.P. told the Ryans.

The man laughed. "You sober enough these days, Savoie?"

Mrs. Ryan flinched, apparently mortified. Then scraped up a set of keys from the mantel and did not look at A.P. "Thank you, dawlin', but you run on. You got your little mama over there, I seen her come in earlier."

"You going to put a shirt on, Kevin?" Ryan belched. "Getting cool out..."

"Bled all over it."

"For God's sake, get him a jacket or something, Eileen!"

A.P. stepped through the door, shut it, then made his unnoticed way outside. *Good thing Kevin's not hurt too bad. Be bleeding to death while that dickhead jerks everybody around...*

He took his time getting to his own place. Lit a cigarette and let Feen wait, postponing the anticlimactic explanation. He'd felt so effective a moment ago. Necessary. Now just mostly embarrassed, having over-reacted to something that wasn't much of anything. *Semi-automatic in one hand, walking cane in the other. Some hero.*

The Ryan car out front started up and pulled away from the curb.

I look ridiculous.

Feen had to come searching for him, opening the door with a hesitant squeak, finding him seated on his own steps not three feet away. If she was angry at having had to endure what had probably been an uneasy wait, she didn't let on. If she'd been worried, she didn't show that either.

All she did was come down the steps and sit down beside him, maybe forgetting the blood there that might still be wet, and her in her good jeans. "I could hear your voice through the wall. No fighting, though. No gunshots…"

"No."

"So everything's okay?"

Mick'd be calling me "Teenage Mutant Ninja Turtle", and Cam'd be laughing with her. "Honestly, Feen, I don't know."

CHAPTER TEN

Rehearsal seemed snake-bit the afternoon of Cam's arrival, with bungled intros and bad tempers. That new percussionist, Laskey, a modern-jazz veteran, was openly resentful of instructions from anybody, even Bee-Bee. Delphine kept a low profile, staying out of A.P.'s way. He appeared on the verge of jumping out of his skin every time she came near enough to hear him mutter, "Somebody kill me."

"Please don't say that."

She'd passed a mop over his kitchen floor back on Tchoupitoulas Street, then vacuumed the front room carpet until it got back some of its original color. With one ear pressed to the telephone receiver and Paul's voice from Bois Sec ("I wouldn't mind seeing Cam, but Mickey's a whole other matter."), she'd ironed the ruffled collar of her best dress and had waited for her son to come out of the bathroom where he'd anointed himself with enough patchouli to sink a barge.

"Traffic around the airport's going to be pure hell," he climbed down off his bar stool now during a brief break, heading for the kitchen where Bee-Bee was arguing with somebody over the phone. "All that *couyon* Christmas shopping..."

Lamar and Kyle were discussing the song list, voices very low.

Delphine could've fallen asleep in this new quiet, if she hadn't been so anxious. She had not slept well at all, the night before.

"You sing?" Laskey suddenly called out to her from his drum kit. "Miz Savoie?"

"Excuse me?" She'd forgotten he was there.

He enunciated very precisely, as if he was speaking to a foreigner or to the deaf. Blue marijuana smoke drifted above his head. "I asked a question: can you sing?"

"I can carry a tune." Delphine didn't know what he wanted. He sounded sort of rude. "But y'all don't want me in your band, for sure."

"You speak French?"

"Yeah."

He nodded. "That thick Coonass accent…"

"Yeah. My ass is all Coon." *He sure doesn't have many social skills.*

"What's the matter with your son?" Laskey jerked his head at the door A.P. had disappeared through.

"His little boy's flying in from New York tonight for Christmas. He's just nervous."

"No. I mean…"

"Oh. Vietnam."

Laskey suddenly patted his own chest, a thump that Delphine wasn't ready for. "First Air Cav, Second Division. –Civilians spat on us when we got home, you know that?"

"Yes. People calling A. P. a baby-killer…" *Yet the only baby he killed was his own little brother.*

The drummer's face was opaque. He sat motionless for a while, looking up only when A.P. returned.

But rehearsal immediately began to run smoother.

* * *

Nothing was smooth out on I-10 later that evening, however, with holiday traffic clogging all the exits for the suburban shopping centers. The Interstate was paved with vehicles, A.P. smacking the steering wheel with one hand.

"We're doing fine," Delphine said, looking at her watch. "Catch them at baggage claim, for sure."

A new red BMW tried to pull out of the access road and wedge itself in front of them. A.P. wrenched his window down, shouting, "Wait your turn, *pote-sac!*"

"Boo—"

He came to a dead stop to allow an aged Chevy with little kids in the back seat to pull into the lane ahead of him.

The red BMW waffled up front. It stopped in front of the Chevy, its driver signaling that he now wanted to get into the left-most lane. A.P. pounded the steering wheel. *"Fis d'putain!"*

Delphine leaned to survey the line of vehicles on their left. "Won't nobody let him in, looks like…"

"Hang onto something," A.P. told her. "I'm going around 'em."

"Coo! You can't pass people on the *right*, boo!"

But the van swung out into the pull-off space on the route's starboard shoulder, wheels off the asphalt on Delphine's side, and bumped berserk down the line of traffic, the man in the BMW yelling vain obscenities. Delphine closed her eyes and gripped her seat. A.P. had no seat belts—a violation of state law.

I'm going to give him some for Christmas, she vowed. *Yes sir.*

* * *

There was no place to park in the short-term lot when they reached the airport well past Cam's arrival time. A.P. pulled up to the curb at the downstairs loading zone. "You're going to have to go in and get them, Feen…"

"Me?" *No way I'm going in that place all by myself and face Mickey Wickham! It's been such a long time, and so much has happened…!*

He was pointing to a sliding glass door where travelers bustled out. "Just go right through there and look for the Delta baggage claim. I'm in a no-parking zone here—I can't leave the van."

"Why don't *I* stay with it, then, and you—?"

"Feen. *Please.*" His eyes went down.

"Hey." She kissed him on the cheek, understanding. "You look nice."

He was in his vintage suit jacket with a clean pair of jeans. He smelled nice, too—all that patchouli. Hair combed, glossy and black as a crow's wing. She squeezed his intact right hand. "Stay here, then, boo. I'll be right back."

She opened the door to climb out, but he pulled her back inside for a moment and hugged her. His heart was running a 5-K.

"We're going to be okay," she told him, hopping out of the van in her high-heeled shoes. She went through the glass doors and did not look back.

It had been just him and her once upon a time, him kicking in her belly after her father'd thrown her out. She'd hitch-hiked to Galliano to stay with her married sister, so pregnant she looked like she'd swallowed a classroom globe. The young welder responsible —Paul Savoie—might be at any shipyard in Louisiana by now, and Louisiana had a lot of shipyards. So Delphine and her baby had boarded a Greyhound bus out of Galliano, hitting the road in a search.

This airport was a zillion times busier than those bus stations all those years ago, and loud Christmas Muzak came over the public address system with gargled flight announcements.

We're going to be okay, she told her son again in her mind, both for this time and for all those other times and other terminals. *We're going to be okay.*

Strangers pushed and shoved, carrying shopping bags and suitcases and glittery holiday things. Children whined. The luggage at the Delta carrousel went around and around. She stood on tiptoe in her uncomfortable shoes, hugging her purse to her side, looking high and low for blonds with small boys. *I bet she brought her mama with her. I bet she brought her boyfriend. I bet she brought her mama AND her boyfriend...*

Maybe they missed their—

She caught those blue eyes too late, too late to get her own face into the right expression. A slim, stunning woman in a knit hat was staring her down.

"*Delphine?*" She dropped a carry-on bag to the floor and engulfed Delphine in a clutch—bulky Mexican sweater under Delphine's startled fingers, soft braless bosom, strong arms locked around Delphine's smallness in a spasm—"Oh my God, it *is* you! Oh my God!"

But how right it felt. Something clogged in Delphine's nose and she hugged Mickey hard, rocking with her in a little dance of reunion, babble babble babble! Overlapping words: *You look so good, cher! It's been so long! How ARE you? You look— I look—We look—*

"Grandmom? Grandmom?" A hand tugged at Delphine's jacket and she blinked down at a small face. Straight light bangs hung over big, sleepy dark eyes.

Mère de Dieu, this is really happening. Those are A.P.'s.

Cam was not much shorter than she was. She swooped down. "*Oh, bébé! Oh 'tit bébé! Oh oh oh—!*"

He hugged her. He smelled like bubblegum. "Where's Dad, Grandmom?"

"Outside with the truck—I mean the van. He couldn't leave the truck—I mean the van." Babble babble babble. *Cam's so* tall! *This* is *Cam, yes? Has to be. Look at those eyes.*

"I'm getting big," he said.

"You sure are, for true!"

"Delphine?" Mickey's face was pink and distracted. "I've got all our stuff here. Bags and all. I guess we can go on outside…"

"Ahh… Your mama didn't come?"

"Couldn't get her away from her bridge club long enough to join us."

So where's Terry Lanzl? Delphine searched the faces of bystanders. "Y'all alone?"

"Yep." The corners of Mickey's mouth went down and then back up.

Coo Lord. The girl has had to come alone. She's scared to death. But she's come anyhow.

It was easy to see why Mickey hadn't backed out of the trip: Cam had her by the arm now and was pulling hard, alert and anxious. "Come *on*, Mom!"

"Pick up your bag, Cameron," his mother reminded him.

"Oh yeah." He ran back to shoulder a small backpack.

"Quick," whispered Mickey into Delphine's ear. "What am I in for?"

"Sober."

"You're kidding."

Cam came trotting back and their conversation halted. He passed them at a dead run and Mickey slipped her trembling hand into Delphine's. "Oh, Delphine... Oh, Delphine..."

"*Mom?*" Cam shrilled from the door, impatient.

She pressed her pale lips together, hat covering all her hair except for a few pale strands sticking out over her ears and collar. No makeup—just exquisite cheekbones and a porcelain complexion, her ears and nose and beautiful mouth as delicate as sea shells. She was the only woman Delphine had ever known who sometimes seemed to think she needed to underplay her beauty.

Her upper lip was perspiry now.

How can this be? Delphine, watching, ached for Mickey's terror. *I do love you, girl. I still do love you, even after what you did to my son. After what he maybe did to you. How can this be?*

They showed their baggage claim checks to the guard and hauled the bags through the door, the three of them. The damp air was turning icy. Taxis honked by.

Mickey glanced at Delphine. "So where's—?"

Cam lunged away from her and went tearing down the sidewalk.

"Cam!" Mickey shouted. "Don't run!"

His small sneakers pounded down the concrete away from them, his backpack bobbing. Light hair blowing. Short arms lifting, opening. He was picking up speed. "*Dad!*"

Delphine spotted A.P. standing by the van outside the door she had entered through. He was expecting them to come out that way. She saw him turn now.

"*Dad! Dad!*" Cam was airborne.

A.P. had just enough time to reach out his arms before the child plowed between them like a cannonball, feet off the ground, hitting him mid-chest. A.P. staggered, then they both went down on the sidewalk in a tangle of arms and legs; and Delphine found herself sprinting madly with Mickey right behind her. *Lord, he's broken that bad hip—he's busted his back—*

But the women heard laughter. The thrashing was happy.

"Hey." Mickey brought Delphine up short some distance away with a hand on her arm. "Hey. He's okay. Let's leave them to themselves for a sec."

Cam tussled and rolled with his father, incoherent. A.P. was trying to sit up but he couldn't do it with both arms locked around the child. He laughed like a boy himself, that unaffected falsetto yipping of his that Delphine rarely heard anymore. It hurt her to hear it now.

"He's ruining his good clothes," was all she could say.

"Mom?" Cam's mouth became an urgent O in his face when he looked over his shoulder. One arm beckoned. "Mom? Mom?"

Mickey moved away from Delphine's side. "He needs help standing, I guess..."

But A.P. stood under his own power, one hand on Cam's shoulder for a crutch. Delphine saw him look up.

Mickey threw back her shoulders and stalked briskly down the cement, hard-heeled cowgirl boots smacking the pavement. "Cameron, you're getting too big to go jumping onto people this way! You'll hurt somebody!"

A.P. stood his ground and watched her come.

The distance between them closed. Delphine couldn't catch what they said to each other, but they didn't say much.

A.P.'s ugly hand crept over the back of Mickey's sweater, meeting up with the other beneath her shoulder blades. Yarn crinkled as his strong arms tightened around her. He leaned his back against the van for support and lifted her off her feet, and then set her back down so that he could bury his face in her neck.

CHAPTER ELEVEN

Delphine did most of the talking as they drove back to the city. "Yonder's my husband's cousin's used car lot," she told Mickey as A.P. kept his attention on the highway. Her finger pointed everywhere. "There's where Allen Fontenot's night club used to be at. Right next to that adult book store."

Mickey sat on the van's carpet in the back, next to a silent Cam. They would've had to half-stand to see the book store. Neither stood. "Might be more interesting if you could ride up front here next to your daddy," Delphine told her grandson, "but it's dangerous without a seat belt."

The van idled at a traffic light. Mickey ruffled her son's pale hair. "Cam's got the shys."

"Stop it, Mom."

"It's nearly ten-thirty. I'll bet you're sleepy, kiddo."

Delphine was pointing again. "Look at all the Christmas lights."

"We have reservations at the Marriott downtown," Mickey yawned, "so y'all can just drop us off there now, if it's not too much trouble. What time you guys want to get together in the morning?"

Delphine turned. "What about supper?"

"Ate on the plane."

Cam finally spoke up. "I thought I was staying with Dad tonight."

Delphine looked at A.P., who was expressionless.

"Adrien?" Mickey leaned forward. "Did you tell Cam he could stay with you tonight?"

"You can *all* stay with me tonight. Got heat and indoor plumbing, and everything..."

Cam was tying his shoelaces into square knots. His head was down, mouth working in and out of a pout. "Okay, you take him, then," said Mickey, voice sounding just as tired and strained as her face looked in the neon, "and I'll meet y'all for breakfast tomorrow morning. What time d'you have to be at work?"

"Not going—boss said I could have tomorrow off, if I come in on Sunday instead."

"So okay, then we can all have breakfast and go see the Superdome together. That okay with everybody?"

A.P. pulled up in front of the Marriott Hotel. "I'm playing Tipitina's tomorrow night..."

"Well? You won't have to be there until—what? Five-thirty? Six?"

He didn't answer. Just made his way to the rear of the van and helped her hand her luggage to a bellman. She strode around to Delphine's side and leaned into the window. "Delphine? I'll see you in the morning, then. We'll talk."

"Yeah. Good."

Cam leaned over Delphine and stuck his head out of the open window so that Mickey could kiss him on the cheek. "Goodnight, pal," she said. "Don't you be keeping these folks up too late, now."

Delphine waved and rolled the window back up. Mickey was already disappearing through the glass doors, long legs carrying her through knots of tourists. Her hat was off and her short light hair flew like a shampoo commercial.

"Well." A.P. started the engine. "That was anticlimactic..."

He dropped the two of them off at his place but kept the engine running. "Look, there's something I got to do, Feen, and I see it can't wait. I'll be back as soon as I can. Y'all go inside and get warm."

"*Now?*" She was going to question him further, but he pulled away from the curb with her still holding onto the door handle. She let go.

Cam waited on the sidewalk, backpack shouldered.

Delphine fumbled for her keys, then took his hand. "Well, come on, boo…"

He stood in the front room while she lit the gas heater in the bathroom. She returned to find him studying the lopsided Christmas tree. "It's crooked," he remarked as she helped him out of his ski parka and hung it on the doorknob. Several wrapped presents under it had his name on them, but he didn't seem interested.

"Yeah. It had a little accident. Here." She brought him a slice of grocery store fruitcake from the kitchen, and he sat on the bed and picked at it with small fingers. "You want anything else to eat, *cher?*"

"What do you call me? 'Sha'?"

"Means, like, 'dear' or 'sweetie'. I can fix you a sandwich…"

He shook his head no. "So this is where Dad lives?"

"Yes."

"It's kind of little. There's nothing to do here."

Her optimism evaporated. "*Mais* yeah, there's just him living here and he's mostly by himself. Doesn't need a lot of room, reading and playing guitar."

"We had a biiiiiiggg apartment when we lived on…" He frowned and thought hard, "East Twelfth Street in Manhattan. Dad loved that place because it was close to the Madison Avenue bus. I was just a baby then. We made ice cream in the bathtub with a churn you put ice in and you turn its handle."

"He's got a TV over there. Click it on if you want to."

Cam eyed the small old set balefully. "No cable."

She glanced at her watch. Time was not passing at all.

"Grandmom? Why does Dad call you 'Feen', instead of 'Mom'?"

"Short for how my name's said: 'Del-*feen*'. Guess that's all he heard people calling me when he was a baby. Call me 'Feen' yourself, if you want to…"

"I don't call my other grandmother by her name, though. Seems weird."

"Then say 'Mamère'—that's what I am to my other grandkids. Here. You like magazines? I got to go get changed…"

He flipped through *Rolling Stone* and then wandered around between kitchen and front room while Delphine put on her nightgown in the bathroom. She came back in her quilted robe and turned on the TV, thick face cream daubed all over her complexion. "There! Ain't I a beauty?"

"You're a lot prettier than my other grandmother."

She grinned, hands on hips. "Lord, what a gallant tongue you got on you! You're a Frenchman for sure!"

He pointed. "There's a gun high on a shelf in that closet…"

"Yeah, and don't go climbing up there. Sit down here and stay out of your daddy's stuff."

He didn't quibble. "Do I look like Dad did, when he was a kid?"

"You've got his eyes." She tweaked a small toe inside his red sock. "You're going to be one heart-breaker when you get big, for sure. Like your *papère* Paul. I met him at a *fais-dodo*—a party some friends gave up in Cut Off—and *coo*, could he dance! My little heart went (she squeezed his toe: *bomp! bomp!*) and I've never been the same since."

"Cut it out!" he laughed. "That tickles! So who're you married to now?"

It took her a minute to answer. She put her hands in her lap, disturbed, feeling a headache coming on. "Still your *papère*…" And got up to search through dresser drawers for anything the child could sleep in, finding something acceptable and throwing it to him. "Here, boo. Put that on for pajamas."

"I've got some in my pack. But wait… Let me wear the shirt… Is it Dad's?"

"Yes."

"Turn around," he said, already squirming out of his clothes, and she did. Then: "Do I have to go to bed now? Before he gets back?"

"No, but he's got a real big day ahead of him. He'll need his sleep."

"He'll sleep good if he's sloshed. –You can turn around now."

She sank onto the bed at the remark, hearing Mickey in it. "Your daddy's not drinking at the moment, Cam—I don't guess anybody realizes that. Except me."

He didn't react. His impenetrable face, too, was Mickey's. "But doesn't he have to? Because he's sick, and it makes him drink?"

"Pills made him sick in the army. Sit down here," she patted a place beside her on the bed. "Who told you this?"

"Mom. He used to yell at Mom sometimes. He was in the hospital once. I was real little—they didn't let me see him." He played with his long shirt tail. "Terry Lanzl's told me a lot about it, too. He's okay. He doesn't treat me like a baby, at least."

She sighed. "Care for some more cake?"

"No, thanks. Terry's not around a whole lot, but he says he likes me. He buys me stuff. Can I stay Cam Savoie, if him and Mom get married? Or will I have to be Cam Lanzl?"

"I don't know." Delphine's headache hit with full force. She found a jar of Motrin by the bed, and washed down two with a Coke.

"Mamère? Does Dad still love Mom?"

She crawled up onto the bed beside him with her Coke and shared it with him, blue. "I don't know. He doesn't tell me much…"

"Why not?"

Those terrible days, Tee-Nick dying and A.P. keeping his own misery secret. "He doesn't want to worry me, I guess."

"Well, he used to really love her—believe it or not—once upon a time. Holding her hand, watching TV or something. But he played with me all the time, too. And sang. Mom says he sang me to sleep when I was a baby. Him and Mom used to get dressed up and go out, if they could find a babysitter. He'd take me to the movies too, just him and me. We'd go to Chinatown on the subway. —He could walk better then, I think."

Delphine had to know: "Well—but when he yelled at her, boo —what was he yelling about?"

"Ohhh..." He blew, and his bangs flew. "*You* know. Asking her if she liked some other guy more than him, stuff like that. But they had sex a lot. I didn't know it was sex—I thought they liked to wrestle—I was real little. But one time, they were yelling at each other about a lady Dad knew and Mom really did hit him. I saw her hit him in the face. *Boy*, ol' Mom can really hit. He didn't hit her back, though. Never. But Terry has. She says he didn't, but I saw it."

Delphine heard A.P.'s key turn in the lock. Cam galloped to the door and held it open while his father dragged his cane and guitar case through. He looked tired and moved stiffly. His tumble at the airport had done him no good. "Y'all still up?"

"Cam wanted to visit with you a little before bedtime..."

"That's good. —Hand me that Motrin, please."

She did, then went into the kitchen for water to swallow it with.

He was face-down on the bed when she returned, Cam astride him, giving him an enthusiastic massage, A.P.'s bare back a patchwork of slick and pink scar tissue beginning just under his left shoulder-blade. He seemed so vulnerable from the rear, Delphine noticed. Exposed, injured, ready for the knife. She looked away.

"What's up with your back, Dad?" Cam said. "I thought it was your legs."

"Yeah, one of 'em's longer than the other now. Gives me a little back-ache sometimes, no big deal." He sat up enough to take the medication from Delphine, then collapsed back into his pillow, one corner of his white smile visible. "I got us some seat belts, y'all. A while ago."

"*Coo!* Where're they at?"

"Jesus! They're in the *van*, Feen!" But he was still smiling. Eyes closed. "From Lamar Legendre's body shop. Installed 'em myself, while Bee-Bee held the work light."

Cam kneaded his father's trapezius muscles, blond hair hanging over his ears and onto his cheeks. "Will Mom and I get to see you play tomorrow night?"

"Don't know. Up to her."

"Don't fall asleep yet, A.P.," said Delphine. "Cam can't get under the covers if you're lying on top of them."

He rolled off and stood while she turned back the fresh sheets and blankets. As she went into the kitchen to prepare her own roll-away bed, she could hear A.P.'s laughter and Cam's happy chatter coming from the front room.

Thank God they know what to do for each other. I don't know what to do for either of them.

* * *

Cam was out cold, nestled against A.P. like a puppy. *My arm's gone to sleep,* thought his father, *but damn if I move it. What a great kid you are, son. But I'll embarrass you, sooner or later. Wish you could've known me back when I was still my old self. No bad habits.*

The self your mother met.

New girl in town, never seen her before—like a fairytale princess—showing up at the marina with her daddy, out of the blue. No warning. Ordinary day. Hotter'n hell.

But here she is. The love of my life, and I know it immediately. Just about giving me a heart attack. Unreal face, skin, body—she ain't even sweating. Long-legged and blond, graceful as a ballerina, no baby-fat on her. No kind of fat at all anywhere, except for those beautiful tits. Where the nipples suddenly jut out against a bra.

And I want to touch them, and I want to kiss them. Her soft mouth is open, and I need to kiss that, too.

"I'M GOING TO MARRY YOU."—Goddam couyon *thing to tell her, but my brain's not working. Only thing that's working's in my crotch.*

Soon as she's gone with her daddy, all I can do is lock up and jack off 'til my hands cramp. Burning up for her, day and night. Don't even know her name.

That's when Tee-Nick started to die, Cam. And you began.

* * *

Mickey dialed Terry's number after checking into her hotel room, even though it was already past midnight on the East Coast. He'd still be up. Expecting her call.

He answered on the first ring.

"Hey, honey." She leaned back into overstuffed, large pillows. "We made it."

His voice was tense. "You sound beat."

"I am." *Why do you never sound soothing, Terry?* "It's late."

"Even later over here. –So how's Cam bearing up?"

"Overwhelmed, I think. They keep speaking French to him—his grandmother, I mean. And they talk so fast, sometimes you can't tell which language it is. She keeps showing him things he has no interest in." *Why does it irritate me, when you mention my child? As if you're trying to stay in my good graces, by just saying Cam's name?*

"Well, *I* had a bitch of a day like you wouldn't believe. Team meeting. You'd have thought it was a fucking funeral…"

My day hasn't been all that great, either, honey. Maybe I'll kick back and order a nightcap from room service, once I'm done here with you. "I'm sorry. This hasn't been a great season for any of you Jets, I know that."

He grunted. "So what kind of shape would you say Adrien's in?"

"Not bad. Not as mobile as he used to be, though."

"I mean *mood*-wise. He hostile?"

"Not that I can detect," she said.

"Well, but you've got to pin him down on the divorce issue." He was putting breath into the phone, like a pervert caller. "Because you can't go on like this, Michelle. Forever in limbo."

She didn't love the heavy breathing. "Yeah. I guess it's time…"

"Acting like he's still got some kind of hold on you. –No Plan B, no room to move, no way to know what your choices are… Goddam it, lose your freedom, you've lost all fucking *dignity*. You deserve your freedom. Tell him."

Freedom? With a dominating personality like you *telling me what I should eat for breakfast?*

74

Worse than my lawyer boyfriend of two years ago, honey. More vehement than that film editor of three years ago, and he was Italian.

He never raised a hand to me.

She sighed deeply. "I'll try to find the right moment…"

"Snow him with legal threats! Fling around 'child custody'— you know all his weak spots. Trailer trash like that, what kind of come-back does he have?"

He's never once lived in a trailer and you haven't met him. "But, Terry —honey—some of this needs to be about *you*, and you need to get some sleep now, okay? That big Bills game coming up on Sunday…?"

"What I need is *relaxation*," he uttered after more grunts. Then a breathy pause. "I'm touching myself. Your voice's making me hot."

"Terry, I'm tired."

"Caress yourself, baby… let's do it over the phone… final game of a shitty season, the shit hits the fan *big-time*… head coach, GM, me—the blame gets spread around. You understand that?"

The last thing I feel right now is sexy.

"—You still there?"

"I'm… here."

"You realize I might get fired? You give one good goddam about that?"

"Terry. Honey. I'm sorry. Of course I care."

"Then can you just stick a finger in yourself and tell me about it, for God's sake?"

How embarrassing. I hope the CIA's not tapping this line.

CHAPTER TWELVE

Mickey was standing rosy and squint-eyed outside the hotel in the cold sun when they stopped to pick her up.

A tour guide showed them through the Superdome with a group of other visitors, mentioning the 400 miles of electrical wiring and 9,000 tons of air conditioning that had gone into the completion of the enormous indoor stadium.

Delphine kept her seat when some of the group scaled the steep steps to higher levels, A.P. and Cam among them. *Coo Lord,* she turned and frowned, watching them climbing higher, wondering if the metal railing would hold should A.P. miss a step and come tumbling down the man-made cliff. Mickey stood off a little way, arms folded.

"We can't build one of these in New York, Mom," Cam told her as the guide showed them the press box. "You know why we can't build one?"

"No money."

"There's no *room* to build one! We'd have to tear down Trump Tower!"

A.P. went over to the gift counter on their way out and bought a bagful of souvenirs, Saints merchandise. Cam hugged it all to his chest, then peeled the backing off a bumper sticker. "Bend down, Mom."

Mickey did as she was asked, and Cam plastered *SAINTS* across the back of her Mexican sweater. "Nobody has a car in New York," he explained to Delphine. "We've never had a car."

Mickey tried to look over her shoulder at the bright plastic on her back.

"Yeah," said A.P., "but that ain't her bumper, man." –Spoken while peeling a second sticker, slapping it onto the seat of her jeans before she noticed what he was up to.

Cam hooted, thrilled. Mickey blushed bright red and spun around.

But A.P. seemed suddenly abashed, as if her laughter was surprising him. As if he'd been expecting something else.

* * *

"A *kite?* In the winter?"

"Yeah, Mom," said Cam. "It's like a big dragon, and it's forty-two feet long. It's one of my Christmas presents—Dad let me unwrap it this morning."

A.P. eyed the women from the driver's seat. "Y'all want to come? We're just going up on the levee, won't be there more than an hour. But I promised him."

"I wish you'd stop promising him things without checking with me," Mickey reminded him. She looked at Delphine.

"*Mais,* somebody's got to fix dinner," Delphine told them. "Y'all go on."

Mickey scrubbed the side of her boot against the curb. "No. Let me stay here."

They watched A.P. and Cam drive off in the van with a dragon kite in it somewhere. "Good Lord," Mickey muttered. "The Mississippi River. Hope they don't fall in…"

Delphine unlocked the apartment door. "No, there's a lot of green space up there. Like a park now. Come on and let's you and me get dinner made. Got us some red beans been soaking all night."

The place smelled smoky but clean. Mickey leaned against the refrigerator, arms hugging herself, studying the peeling ceiling and a cracked window repaired with duct tape. "You know how *smart* that man is, Delphine? Do you know what a *waste* I see here?"

"Who we talking about?"

"Adrien."

"Oh. Well…" She started the rice.

"So what can I help you do? I still know my way around a Louisiana kitchen, I think."

"Some onion needs chopping. Look down there in the fridge bottom."

Delphine heard the refrigerator door open. Then: "Is he seeing anybody?"

"A.P.?" She handed Mickey a small knife and a plate to cut upon. "No. Well, I find stuff like pantyhose in here, sometimes. But nothing regular. Nothing that lasts. They come and they go."

Mickey seated herself at the table and began chopping. Flicked an onion skin from her wrist. "I think that's his true pattern, unfortunately… monogamy as alien to him as flight… he was like that back in high school, girls out the ying-yang. And him the happiest person I'd ever met in my whole life, which doesn't seem at all *fair*…"

You sure changed that. Delphine silently shook her head.

Mickey sighed. "I used to think his war injuries would slow him down, silly me. He had a whole series of girl friends while I was away in Yucatán doing my field work—which I guess was okay then, because we'd broken up. But silly me, we got back together. I figured *marriage* would slow him down. Fatherhood. Even alcohol —most alcoholics are impotent. Lord, Lord. Silly me."

"But maybe it's *because* he's crippled? Maybe he's got to prove something?"

"Maybe. Hell. –So what's the VA telling him, these days?"

A shrug. "I don't know. He sure needs Motrin…"

"And probably another hip replacement." Mickey stood. "So where d'you want me to put these onions?"

"Right here in the skillet with the sausage, thanks." Delphine sautéed. The sausage sizzled and the onions began to turn transparent. "So what about you? You're engaged?"

"Lord, *no.*" She didn't speak the expected name. "I'm seeing somebody, yes, but it's not too serious yet. He's on the staff of the New York Jets and they're playing their final game of the season this weekend—that's why he couldn't come. I don't know if it's going anywhere, our relationship. And if we break up, I sorta worry about Cam. He's attached to him."

Delphine recalled last night's conversation. *Maybe not.*

* * *

It was as windy as ever up on the levee here. Wind blew even on the hottest days, when breezes were humid blasts. *Maybe it's because the land's higher here than anywhere else around,* A.P. thought now. *Or maybe there's just something about a wide river that draws it. Like a lake. Like the sea.*

Ought to look for a book about it…

Clouds blew past overhead, holes in them sending patches of sunlight sweeping across the open ground like spotlights. One of these found Cam now and lit him like a circus performer as he stood in the wind and clutched the spooled kite string. His light hair shone.

A.P. sat on the tan winter grass near the parked van and smoked, legs stretched out, curly hair whipping. Cam glanced over his shoulder and waved showily. Posing like a Saturday morning cartoon hero, self-conscious. *Hilarious as hell, but you can't let your kid see you laughing at him.*

"Look, Dad! It's going into outer space!"

The kite climbed, long tail creating arcs in the stiff breeze, bright transparent plastic body navigating the sky in stained-glass colors. *Looks more like some giant sperm cell than a dragon.* A.P. cupped his hands around his mouth, then shouted after a moment, "Be careful you don't lose it! Lot of stress on that string!"

Cam nodded, making an OK with finger and thumb. And fumbled the big wooden spool. String whirred off it in a blur as it fell, sending it spinning and bumping along the grass with Cam two steps behind it. A.P. felt his son's embarrassment—*space pilot's took a nose dive*—but had to laugh gently at the child's buzzard luck. "Grab it! Grab it!"

A woman jogged by down the levee with an Irish setter, and the dog wheeled when it saw the spool bumping past. Stretching out in pure speed, it raked up the object in its mouth before Cam could overtake either. "*Hey!*" he yelled, outraged.

A.P. got to his feet with his cane and started over the grass, wind tossing his hair and pulling at his jacket. *Everybody just needs to be patient for a little bit, and the dog'll get tired of it. Chasing him around like this'll only jack him up.* "Cam? Come here a sec, son…"

The setter swooped by Cam again with the spool in its drooling mouth, its body near flat as it turned in tight, mad circles. Cam made a lunge. Missed. The dog ran to the levee's edge, disappearing over the bank where low willows grew. A freighter flying the Portuguese flag glided past, way out on the wide gray water.

"*Cam?*" A.P. began to run.

The child never looked back. He took hold of a nearby willow branch and crouched. Then his shoulders hunched, and he went over the edge and was gone.

A.P. flailed with arms and cane, hopping on his semi-good leg when he reached the bank, eyes watering but brain lucid with slow-motion adrenaline. He wiped with a cuff to clear his vision, dropping backwards onto his buttocks to slide feet-first halfway down the slope, finally grabbing a sapling stump with one hand to stop himself. The bank fell maybe ten more feet in an uneven rough incline. The river level was low. He dropped another frantic five feet where his body caught in brush.

A sand bar of mud, broken glass, and old tires jutted out from the levee into shallow swirling water where wavelets from the wake of the passing ship slapped at rusted metal detritus. The dog splashed and barked twenty yards upriver. But Cam stood amid the trash, the seat of his jeans muddy, winding string back onto the recovered spool. He saw A.P. there above him, shaded his eyes for a moment, then turned and began to climb his way back up the steep bank. Glum. "String broke, Dad. Stupid dog. Kite's flown off to Antarctica, I guess…"

A.P. sat there wedged into root systems and slippery mud, hip and leg and back on fire, receding adrenaline becoming the retro-panic shakes. He reached down a hand, and Cam took hold of it. A.P. pulled and dragged Cam higher, but then kept on pulling and pulling, scrambling for heel holds with his Adidas—with fury—hauling Cam up the bank until it seemed that both of their arms might dislocate.

He got them both over the edge onto the mown tan grass and then flipped Cam over his thighs and whacked him twice on the bottom before the child could roll over and off. He smacked him a third time as Cam dodged, but he had a blue-collar grip on the boy's wrist and Cam could not break free. "Look at me, son," he ordered after a while in a low voice, seeing Cam's chest heave and his face become red. "Look up here a minute."

Cam began to sob, shackled. "I hate you! I hate you!"

"You can hate me if you want to, son, but I'm not going to let you kill yourself for no damn *kite*."

Little fingers clawed at the hand holding the wrist. "You *hurt* me!"

"Look up here, son. Look at me." A.P. waited, gentler now. "You hurt me, too. Look up here for a minute, Cam."

Cam tossed his head to one side and another, but finally raised it. He sniffled, then turned a skeptical face up to A.P., who was pointing at his own eyes. "Look, Cam. You see it?"

"Are you crying?" he asked after a long moment.

A.P. smiled, rubbing a hand across his face. "No. But I can't run. Hurts like hell when I try these days. Makes my eyes water."

"Does it still hurt like hell now?"

"It's easing off. Give me a minute. I'll be able to stand up in a minute or two. Let's just sit here for now." He pulled the child against his chest, pressing his chin down on top of the light hair. Cam's arms went around him after a while. They watched the wide river flow by with logs in its current. Little puckers patterned its surface, and when he felt water running down the back of his neck, he noticed that it was raining.

Pulling his jacket up and over Cam's back to keep him dry, he said "Cam, there's a lot of things I can't do. I don't know if I can fish you out of a river."

"Can you swim?"

The rain soaked into his hair. "I don't know. I used to could."

Both of them were wet and muddy when they got back to the van. "Our moms are going to kill us," said Cam. "Do we have to go back now?"

"I got to be at Tipitina's by six." Water was filling the street gutters where the grates were choked with leaves. "Probably won't nobody come out in weather like this, though, and it so close to Christmas. We'll probably be the only ones there."

Cam was serious. "So what'll you do? If no audience comes?"

"Play video games." A.P. laughed. Then laughed harder, when he recognized it as the truth. "You and me and the guys, we'll just chill and play video games with Frieda Washington."

"But then I won't get to hear you!"

"No great loss." He turned onto Tchoupitoulas Street and slowed to pull up at the curb, conscious of fatigue and depression. He knew where the fatigue came from. The depression had just come down like the rain. He killed the engine, then leaned back in the seat, hands in his lap. "Look, Cam. I'm not all that *good*, son. So don't expect anything like on *MTV*. You know what I'm saying?"

The house where he lived stood dilapidated in the drizzle. That weathered apartment door in the alley seemed a long way away. *I used to have an umbrella—don't know what's happened to it. I used to have lots of things I don't have anymore.*

"*I* know!" Cam was suddenly inspired. "Why don't we let *my* mom yell at you, and *your* mom yell at *me*?"

Muddy jeans. Sodden sneakers—invitations to strep viruses, and other winter-weather bugs. "Cam, your mom's definitely going to ream me out, no matter what."

CHAPTER THIRTEEN

Delphine took Cam's hand and stepped up to the young man collecting cover charges at the door. Taped music pounded. "I'm—"

"Sorry, ma'am." He waved somebody else's ten-dollar bill at Cam. "He's underage."

"He'll stick to Coca-Cola."

The kid's head shook a busy *No*. "State law. Has to have I.D. saying he's twenty-one."

"I *told* Adrien!" Mickey whispered to Delphine. "I *told* him!"

Delphine drew herself up. "*Mais* look, son. I'm Mrs. Paul Savoie—"

"I'm Mrs. *A.P.* Savoie." Mickey stepped in front of her, with as steely a smile as ever her late oil-executive father could have mustered. "And we have complimentary reservations."

Delphine couldn't see the stage but she could hear random notes from Kyle's bass. The moneyman pulled at the skirt of a neo-hippie waitress. "Hey, Meg—Go ask Mr. Legendre if he knows anything about—"

"Mr. *Walter* Legendre: Bee-Bee." Delphine took the girl by an elbow. "Please tell him the Savoies are here..."

But a short flat-topped Afro already loomed over her head, Bee-Bee's single black eye glittering next to the eyepatch. He stood unmoved in the press and shove, immobile as a rock in a tide while the crowd surged past him. "Where y'all been? Your table's this way."

Mickey looked at Delphine and held Cam close by the shoulders. "Hard time getting a cab," said Delphine. "This terrible rain…"

"Pleasure to meet you, Mickey Savoie." Bee-Bee took her and steered her through the crowd, Cam and Delphine right behind, up to an empty table near the stage's very edge where the band's instruments and microphones waited, A.P.'s guitar resting next to a bar stool. Bee-Bee pulled out chairs for both women, then bent down eye-to-eye with Cam. "How you doing, son?"

"Fine." Cam was shy, head down.

"Can't talk now, almost show-time." He straightened. "See y'all after the first set. Enjoy yourselves."

Mickey watched him go. "So that's Rasputin, I take it?"

Cam looked at her. "What's 'rasputing'?"

Laughing, she just shook her head and signaled a waitress to order drinks. *Just so lovely,* Delphine marveled at Mickey. *Lipstick and eyeshadow, hair all gelled tonight like some fashion model's, I'd be feeling* beaucoup *old and ugly if I wasn't so proud to be seen with her.*

The girl went off for Mickey's whiskey sour, Cam's Coke, and Delphine's vodka stinger. Approvingly, Delphine was turning her head in all directions to view everything. The space was impressive, roomier than she'd expected, and it was jammed. Frieda Washington had brought in a capacity crowd on this bad, wet night. Charles Neville was two tables away, and jazz guitar great Steve Masakowski and wife Ulrike were in conversation with onlookers at the bar. A genial, overweight actor from movies and TV—John Goodman—was with a tableful of laughing people, and she tried not to stare at him. *But coo Lord, staring's half the fun.*

A.P. and his band mates showed up onstage one by one, individually taking their places with nonchalance, chatting inaudibly, getting comfortable among their instruments. Delphine tried to catch her son's eye as he slung his guitar over his shoulder and took his own seat on the tall stool, but he didn't look down at their table. What occupied him was manipulating the microphone to a good level in front of his mouth. The audience continued to loudly converse.

"Ladies and gentlemen," Bee-Bee's sudden voice interrupted everybody over the sound system, right on time, "we present for your listening pleasure tonight, New Orleans' own A.P. Savoie and the No-Frills Band."

House lights went down, stage lights came up, and a keyboard intro spoke from the amps. Cam popped up onto his feet and stood. *Anna Banana!* Delphine almost cheered.

Laskey's new percussion was making it a mambo, and Cam began to dance next to Mickey's chair, covering his ears and grinning maniacally at Delphine. His mother tugged at his arm. *"Sit down!"*

A.P. had never once looked directly at them but Delphine knew he felt them there because his good hand shook when he seized the mike.

But his voice did not. It slid out like oil when he jammed the microphone resolutely to his chin. Then he took his hand away, put pick to guitar strings, and jerked both shoulders to kick in the total big sound. The crowd made noise but he kept his eyes on the lights as if God lived up there. "Anna, Anna / Heard you practice on banana?" His sudden dimpled smile flashed, white teeth, dented cheeks. "If I'm real, real good / Would you practice on *me?*"

"Jesus!" Mickey mouthed, unheard. Chairs scraped as couples jumped to their feet to dance between the tables, drinks in their hands.

The number ended in whistles and shouts, people's fists in the air. Cam jumped up onto his chair, arms spread wide. Mickey didn't tell him to sit down.

A.P. gave his audience no time to cool off, Laskey's rhythm rolling on into a Cajun two-step this time, *Long Tall Sally* sung in French—eliciting laughter when A.P. forgot the lyrics, whooped and doubled over with mirth, smacking his forehead and switching to instant English. To cheers from everywhere, people beginning to sing along with him, migrating from the bar, from out front, from the kitchen, from the bathrooms, drawn as close to the stage as they could get for whatever was happening here. Nobody seemed to be sure exactly what it was, except it was Something. Here was *Somebody.*

Here and now.

"I want to take y'all back," A.P. told them conversationally, as if they were all merely guests on his family's *galerie*, "to your first real love. And I'm not talking about no *car...*"

Right in the palm of his hand, Delphine realized. *He's got 'em all in the palm of his hand.*

"...I'm not talking about no Mustang or Dodge Charger, I'm not talking dogs, cats, football, or that beer you had to lie to buy. I'm talking *girl.*"

An inarticulate roar answered him.

"I'm talking," he scratched his chin, sliding off his bar stool to stand, "about trying to get *laid.* I'm talking about holding my girl and telling her how I feel about her. Telling her how I feel, so I can get *laid.*"

Huge laugh.

"But also telling her how I feel... because it's just how I feel." He lowered his head—a reggae, this time:

"Dancing with the one I love 'til quarter of three,
I can't believe a girl like you is dancing with me.
Put your arms around me as the radio plays.
Give us something to remember in our cooling-off days.

I really really love you and I'm out of control.
You give your precious body, and I'll give you my soul.
Cure my loving fever, girl, I'll show you the ways,
And the memory will warm us in our cooling-off days..."

"Mom?" Cam was pulling at Mickey's sweater. "*Mom?*"

Delphine saw Mickey's hands had covered her face. They fluttered down again like two white wings.

Bodies pressed against the stage. Delphine had to get to her feet to see over their heads now, and she held Cam's legs as he stood on his chair.

A.P. swayed on his muddy Adidas above all the heads and arms and beers, beads of sweat like tiny ornaments hanging from the wild ends of his hair, head back and eyes closed, entranced and entrancing.

Where was Mickey now? Delphine tried to see. Mickey still sat, low and hidden, arms wrapped around herself, head down.

He introduced the band members to astounding applause for each, then their set ended in one more number, Gershwin's *Of Thee I Sing* done as New Orleans funk. After which No-Frills left the stage while their audience went psycho, but no encore was forthcoming. The house lights came back up and the mob down front finally dispersed in a grumbling shuffle. Existence became normal again.

Cam flopped back onto his seat and fanned himself with his open hand, drained and happily disoriented. "Where's Mom?"

Delphine turned, her ears ringing, slightly dizzy herself. "I... don't know. Maybe the bathroom."

She swiveled her head back around and there was A.P., pulling up a chair just like an ordinary person. Cam pounced: "Dad! Dad! Give me your autograph!"

He took Cam into a one-armed hug and pulled Delphine in with the other. She felt his heart racing. Strangers moved past the three of them to the bar, many of them pausing to pound A.P. on the back—"Dynamite!" "Terrific!" "Marry me!"

"Where'd Mick get to?" He let Delphine go, took out his Zippo and lit a smoke.

But a pale hand took shape on his damp shoulder. Mickey had come up behind him, and he reached up and patted her fingers.

"Hi." She bent to kiss the top of his head, another whiskey sour in her hand. "You were pretty good, pal. Proud of ya!"

Delphine made room for her at the table, but she didn't sit. Just studied her watch. "How long will Frieda Washington perform, Adrien?"

"Longer than us."

"Well, I've got to get Cam back to the hotel, but I'd kind of like to meet the No-Frillers, and then maybe Cam and I can hear a little of her, before—?"

"Sure." He stood, obviously surprised and pleased, and all four of them went in search of the band. A couple introduced as Mike and Carla Maggio hugged A.P. and congratulated him.

Bee-Bee turned up at the bar with a white man who was wearing diamond pinky rings. His own fingers peeled the label off a beer bottle as he chewed a sodden cigar and listened to whatever his companion was saying. No introductions were made.

Kyle, Lamar, and Laskey were backstage, all of them upbeat, smoking and laughing at nothing. Loud music came from out front. Frieda Washington was beginning her set.

"We'd better get back, y'all," said Delphine. "Somebody's going to get our table."

Nobody moved. Mickey was on her third whiskey sour, standing easy under A.P.'s draping arm, enchanting his band mates: "Oh, I'm in the Anthro department at NYU... nothing glamorous..." She was heel-and-toe, heel-and-toe, her boots making a deprecatory little dance on the floor, "and I'm not musical *at all*... I wrote my dissertation on matrilineal descent among the Maya in Yucatán, but now I'm teaching—"

Delphine tuned out. Looked at Cam. "You sleepy, boo?"

"Are you kidding?"

"Your mom's talking shop. You want to go hear Frieda?"

"Are you *kidding*?"

"We're going to have to stand in back though, I guess. Bet you our table's gone."

* * *

"Let's get it over with," Mickey found herself saying to Adrien as they went out front again. "Now's the time, pal..."

He jostled her shoulder, happy. She caught the scent of patchouli. "For what?"

"A summit conference, or whatever. You keep telling Cam he

can do stuff. I keep telling him he can't. We're facing a problematic Christmas, if we don't get on the same—"

"*Shit!*" He goggled at a throng of usurpers. "Our *maudit* table's gone...!"

"As if we could hear each other out here," she had to shout.

She saw him considering Bee-Bee's intense conversation with the stranger, still ongoing at the bar. "But I got another show to do tonight, babe. This isn't the best time to get into a hassle..."

"No hassle. Let's just establish *détente.* How long've we got?"

He consulted his watch. "About an hour, max."

"Well, I can't make it through the next few days unless we can normalize things, Adrien. Aren't you tired of thinking I'm a monster?"

He interrupted Bee-Bee's conference with the merest touch on his shoulder. "We're going somewhere a little quieter for a minute, Beeb. Be back in plenty of time for the second set."

Bee-Bee just nodded, frowning. *He's sure no barrel of laughs,* Mickey sighed.

They made their way nearer the front door where the rain seemed to be slacking up a little on the other side of the glass. It was less noisy here, at least. Mickey pointed at the rear of the crowd. "Look."

Delphine and Cam were dancing with their backs to the bar, both of them unself-conscious and enthusiastic. Adrien grinned at Mickey and she had to smile back, realizing that they were the only two people on earth who could see Delphine and Cam dancing together and enjoy exactly the same thoughts about it.

His good hand beat time on top of the cigarette machine, articulate, long-fingered. *I used to hold his hands and rub my fingertips over those veins and think about how his blood and mine would someday flow through a child. My hair would stand on end with the pleasure of it.*

"So let's talk," he said. "Should we go backstage again?"

She shook her head. "Music's just as loud back there..."

"Okay," he stuck a hand into his pocket after a moment and pulled out a jangling set of keys, "but it's still drizzling outside. You got an umbrella, or something?"

"Nope." *We haven't been alone together in years. He comes up to see Cam, and then there's Cam and Mama and my friends. Everybody all hovering around to keep us cheerful and friendly. As if I were going to knife him in an unguarded moment.*

Or he me.

"A little rain won't melt us," she said.

Trying to shelter her with an arm, juggling his cane, he helped her out the door. "*Mais* no. Come on."

They didn't run—she didn't expect him to try—but hardly any rain fell now, thank God. The van was parked with its rear nearest the building and her gelled hair wasn't terribly sticky by the time he got the back door unlocked. She crawled inside and he followed, pulling himself forward on his hands. Then it was she who reached out for the door and swung it shut with a hollow clang. The van's interior was dark, smelling of stale smoke and patchouli.

Adrien maneuvered past her to the driver's seat. "You want to just ride around, or go someplace for coffee?"

But she was wet enough to be chilly. "Just turn on the heater, and we can... you know..."

"Heater don't work." He helped her into the passenger seat up front. "But the radio does..."

I wish I wasn't so drunk. I'm liable to discuss Terry. Pour my guts out about this relationship I don't know how to get out of.

He rubbed the cold damp yarn at her shoulder. "Well?"

She felt idiotic. She was onto herself. She knew what she was doing, and she knew that Adrien knew it, too. Those fingers of his brushed her cheek—tentative, something that could be interpreted as an accident. She could ignore it if she wanted to. "So how've you been, Mick?"

"I've been okay."

A pause. "That's *it*? 'I've been okay'? We risk pneumonia coming out here so you could say that?"

She laughed.

"And you're looking extra-gorgeous tonight. –For the public in general, or a specific individual, possibly?"

Nothing I can say. He knows the answer anyway.

And yes, he did. Leaning across the gear shift, cradling her head in the palm of his good hand, he gave her a deep kiss right into her ear. There was no way to ignore something like that.

They thrashed their way into the back, unfastening and unzipping, Mickey softly laughing, "Are you making a pass at me, pal?"

"Beat me! Whip me!" She could feel him smiling against her neck. "Make me feel cheap. Make me write bad checks."

Wonderful French kisses. In his genes.

And in his other jeans, my Good Ol' Friend. "Oh, Jesus—you could hit home runs with this thing… Get a condom on, get a condom, get a condom…"

"Okay, here… Play ball…"

Just like old times: Michelle Wickham and Adrien Paul Savoie, swinging for the fences. She kissed his eyelids, his chin, his lips. "Oh, just fuck me senseless!"

He could still do it. Nail her to the floor. Effortlessly reaching her G-spot—and H-spot and even I-spot, and everything in between—hung like a god.

"Oh my sweet love, that's *so* good. That's *so* good. That's *so* good…"

"Getting old, babe. Don't expect no immediate encore…"

Pulling his head down into her breasts, stroking his damp hair, she fingered the little gold earring. No ring finger, but she'd bought him a wedding band anyway. Had it melted and reshaped, then pierced his ear herself and put it in.

He still wore it.

Lord, how many years ago did I take off my own? Do I even know where it is?

"So when're we getting divorced?" he asked her.

Intoxicated with patchouli, she'd been thinking *I'm remembering why I married this man. "Divorced?" Why is it again I'm divorcing this man?* "Well, I haven't been in that much of a hurry, actually, to legalize anything yet. Because it seems to me that Cam—"

"You just find it convenient to tell potential lovers you're married."

She thought about that. "Well. Yes."

"I'm not condemning you, babe. I do the same thing."

Terry'd punch me in the stomach if he could see me now. "Beat me! Whip me!"—not funny, not with Terry. All those steroids he claims he isn't taking. All that cocaine he scores from his glamorous pro pals.

They nodded at the guy collecting cover charges at the door, pushing past the queue of audience coming in for the second set. But Mickey halted near the bar, just outside the ladies' room, holding Adrien by the arm. "Wait—I'm a *wreck*, pal—look at me! I need to go in here and get myself tidied up, before I collect Cam…"

"Stay with me tonight." He stepped in closer, mouth not six inches from hers. "Let Delphine and Cam have the hotel room."

She wiped lipstick off his face with a tissue. "Yes, but Terry's going to call me there. He knows I'm married, but he's still going to call."

Sleepy eyes regarded her without judgment, two big dark pools she could fall into. She wanted to kiss them shut so they wouldn't be making things happen so fucking *fast*.

Lined-up bystanders were recognizing him, watching both of them. Mickey became embarrassed when she noticed. "Just let me get cleaned up, pal—I'll talk to you tomorrow, I promise—and we might be able to arrange something for tomorrow night after your show. But I need to go in here *right now*, get Cam, then call a cab for the Marriott. That's tonight's plan. Okay?"

His slow kiss said *Okay*. It said *Fine*. It said *I'll hold you to it*.

But she had second thoughts after he pressed her hand, when he smiled that dented smile of his and nodded, then went limping away through the strangers with his silver-headed cane. *Dammit*, she thought, watching him go, those slim damaged hips so easy to wrap her legs around, *tomorrow night's such a long way away…*

So suppose it's Delphine who spends tonight with Cam? She doesn't live a life of luxury—she'd love the Marriott. I can call Terry from Adrien's apartment, head him off at the pass. Important final game on Sunday, he might not even be home. And it's not like I'm taking Adrien back, this doesn't have to be anything serious, Mickey told her own increasingly excited reflection as she repaired her appearance in the ladies' room, smelling his patchouli on her body, feeling her nipples erect. *But maybe we can see where it leads. It might not lead anywhere. But...*

She emerged from the ladies' room and went in search of her menfolks. Adrien was the one she spotted first.

He never saw her, and obviously wasn't expecting to. His back turned, he was at a table covered in dirty glasses with a redhead toweling his hair dry. "Hey, don't pull it all out, Kirsten," he pleaded, laughing.

"But you could use a personal trainer, just look at you!" she answered with giggles, big boobs jiggling in her low-cut neckline. "And you owe me a rematch, by the way..."

"What at?"

"You know what at!"

Lord God, I'm a fool.

* * *

Delphine should've been sleeping better than this. Tipitina's had been a triumph. And all the dancing she'd enjoyed with Cam should've worn her out. That vodka stinger, too, had been relaxing. The rain had stopped. It was very late. *Or very early,* she thought. *Depends on how you look at it.*

But she couldn't get comfortable on her roll-away bed now, and whenever she turned over, or tried to fluff her pillow, she knew she was making noise that might disturb A.P. in the front room. He didn't seem wakeful—she registered his deep, regular breaths whenever she could lie still long enough to hear anything besides the relentless squeaking of the springs and metal legs supporting her. *He's got to get up soon and go to that damn job of his, and Cam's not here to be impressed that he's even got one.*

Rubbing at her weary eyes would only send face cream into them. *Maybe it's time I switched to decaf. I'm getting to that age...*

The sky was lighter when she finally fell asleep.

What she saw was Tee-Nick standing over A.P.'s bleeding body near a Christmas tree, the child's little empty hands, curly dark hair, the tender back of his neck. He turned around and made eye contact with Delphine, and said without expression, "Ho ho ho."

CHAPTER FOURTEEN

Nobody was at A.P.'s apartment when he got off from work the next day, not even Feen.

"Who was that gorgeous blond kept hanging all over you last night?" had been Mike Maggio's sole good-morning when A.P. arrived on time at the record store, groggy but happy.

"My wife." And it had waked him up to be able to give that answer on this busy Saturday. He savored the word now, *wife*, a suspicion of pride in that long *I* vowel. "My wife," he'd repeated, satisfied down to his marrow. Taking several pencils into the stock room and sharpening them one after another, pleased with the wood smell and the precision of the points.

Get her over at my place tonight after the show, out of the rain and in a real bed, get her a little loaded again and put, like, Sinatra on the stereo...

The work day flew by, harried customers snapping up Christmas albums by artists who probably didn't observe Christmas —Barbra Streisand, Neil Diamond—but what did it matter? Nobody seemed to be happy except kids; so many adults in bad moods just in general. But A.P. wasn't among them. What he sang to himself as he drove home was *Joy To The World*, its melody, while he imagined proper accompanying harmony. But then switching, singing the harmony part to the melody playing in his mind. *Joy. To. The. World.*

Maybe he could catch a nap before anybody else got here. It had become colder after last night's showers and he saw his breath. He hadn't bought any kind of Christmas present for Mickey yet because he hadn't thought she'd want anything from him, but now it seemed like the right idea. *It's Christmas—stores're open on Sundays, I'll get her something tomorrow on my way home from work. When I'll know more. After tonight. About what to get her.*

Feen's cosmetics and tooth brush were still in the bathroom, but her shoes and coat and purse were gone. A.P. lit the gas heater near the bed and stood over it for a while, singing *Cooling-off Days* and facing the window, hearing migrating whistling ducks passing overhead and thinking about what a fine view he had of the twilight sky.

We don't seem to've cooled off at all, her and me.

So where do we go for Santa Claus? No chimney here. Cam's too old for that, anyway. Feen'll have to be in Bois Sec. So maybe I ought to take Mickey and Cam to some kind of restaurant on Christmas Eve. If any are open.

Benihana? he laughed. Remembering Mick's willowy body, heat on the backs of his thighs, he got hard in his jeans. *Wouldn't be a big deal to her, but Cam might like it.*

Still in his jacket, he finally sat down on the bed and huddled against the pillows on top of the spread, with a Robertson Davies novel from the public library and the telephone answering machine on. Just in case he fell asleep. Because it was almost dark.

Someone knocked at the door at six-thirty, and he knew it was Feen and Cam—and plugged in the Christmas tree for them—but there stood Bee-Bee on the stoop.

"Getting cold out," he said, as A.P. stepped back to let him inside.

"Yeah, how you doing?"

Bee-Bee pulled up a chair as close to the gas heater as he could get, straddling it backwards, chin propped wearily upon the ladder back. Looking like he'd just run a marathon.

"Care for some coffee?" A.P. remained standing.

Bee-Bee nodded agreement, removing his gloves. An eyebrow

crawled up from out of the eyepatch as he accepted the hot cup. "Savoie, we got us a problem."

A.P. looked at him over the rim of his own.

"You remember me talking to that white man last night...?"

"Yes."

"Name Coley Sanchez-Wilson—Frieda's agent. At Hightower Creative Management in L.A. She been down on her luck some, the last few years. Liking her wine a little too much to suit some folks."

A.P. lit a cigarette. "Lot of that going around..."

"Well," Bee-Bee drained his cup and leaned his cigar into the Zippo's flame, "Frieda went out, got herself some Jesus and rehab. Sanchez-Wilson booking her on a comeback tour..."

"Yes. Happy for her."

Bee-Bee breathed smoke, then frowned at his cigar as if it had burned him. "Wants our band."

A.P. watched. His visitor wasn't smiling, but then he hardly ever did.

"Old label dumped her a few years back, but she's signed with MCA now—Sanchez-Wilson's doing. Getting her on the road, recording live performances. Release a *Frieda Live!* album with the best of it, No-Frills backing her up..."

"Well." A.P. felt yesterday's vague depression settling on him again like frost. He pulled the collar of his jacket up close around his jaws. "You know what you're doing, but I've got to say I'm not real wild about going on the road to back up anybody. I've backed up a lotta-lotta people..."

"Savoie—"

"...but if this is what it takes to get an album out, then maybe we ought to talk it over with the guys. It'd certainly be national exposure, yeah. —I guess I can't think of any real problem..."

"Think *hard*."

He knew. He could see it in the way Bee-Bee's chin drooped on the chair back. The man's jaws barely moved. He said it with mostly lips: "They ain't wanting *you*. They ain't wanting *me*. I call that a problem."

The room was like a meat locker. A.P. glanced at the heater but its flames were blue and steady. He rubbed the stumps of his missing fingers.

"Been talking to Sanchez-Wilson all day. Frieda ain't about to share no spotlight with *you*, Savoie, not even if you're just back-up. Not after you upstaged her. Half the audience left after we finished your second set. Just went home, and there she was. Not happy."

Baffled, A.P. could only throw his hands up. "Nothing personal, I didn't mean to *upstage* anybody, never once crossed my mind!"

"Yeah. Well, we in Diva-World."

"But they still need you to run sound for 'em, Beeb, don't they? As well as produce the album?—*hell!*—you've got credentials, experience, that hit record with Lamar…?"

"Sam Levine producing the album: Frieda Washington On a Come-Back Tour—*Rolling Stone* headline, right there." He began to tick off items on his fingers: "They got Levine. Got an MCA contract. Even got Jesus. All they need now is a kick-ass band. Looks like I done built them one."

A.P. checked his watch. It was almost seven, everything rocketing right into the toilet. "But he's just an agent, this guy? Can he do this? Offer all this? In whose name?"

"Beats me. MCA, I guess. Shit, he already talking to the others this morning, I don't have no contract with none of them. Lamar —he settled in here, got wife and kids and all, and that body shop. But I don't know. I just don't know."

Nightmare. Maybe I'm asleep, and this is all a bad dream. "He's your brother, Beeb. He won't want to see you disrespected."

"No disrespect in making a dollar."

"Okay, look—you saying to me 'Stay humble' all the time, I listen. Been good advice. I don't know how to be a rock star and you've taught me to just be myself onstage, and it must've worked because it's brought us this far. Frieda Washington jealous! Of *me!* Wow, that's just unbelievable! So I have to trust the shit out of you, Beeb, you give me no choice. You know what you're doing, *podna.* I'm your side-kick. So just tell me what you want. We can start all over with new people."

"*Fuck.* If I knew what I was doing, shit'd quit happening to me." Bee-Bee rubbed his face with both hands. Then: *"SHIT SHIT SHIT SHIT!"*, and he fast-balled his coffee at the wall. He threw A.P.'s, as well. One of the cups bounced off with a big wet brown splash all over the paint and carpet, but the other broke into pieces.

"I'm calling the cops, Savoie!" came the inevitable landlord shout from the other half of the shotgun double.

Veins stood out on Bee-Bee's dark neck when he challenged the voice, mouth aimed directly at the plaster board. *"You do that, motherfucker, Ima stomp your ass!"*

A.P. staggered off to the kitchen for clean-up material. *Now I'm evicted, on top of everything else.*

When he returned with a broom and a wad of paper towels, Bee-Bee was already on his hands and fleshy knees, plucking ceramic shards out of the carpet with beige-on-brown fingertips. "Can't use no broom on no carpet, Savoie—didn't your little mama teach you nothing?"

"Move over, you're going to cut yourself. Let me pick it up with these here." *Or let it stay 'til Cam comes, it's not like I give a fuck.*

Bee-Bee stood heavily. "Well. Let me go. Got to get cleaned up before the show."

"Yeah."

"You going to be okay tonight?"

"Yeah, I'm fine."

"I wouldn't have told you right before a show like this, understand, but—"

"Yeah. Thanks for coming by, Beeb. I'd rather hear it this way than wondering why everybody's acting like I got super-contagious swine flu..."

"Let's just do two rock-solid sets." He opened the door. "Flame out with class."

"You got it."

The gate clanged at the end of the alley with Bee-Bee's passage. A.P. sank down again on the bed and smoked and watched the Christmas tree lights sparkle. He did this until he couldn't do it any longer. And then he cried.

* * *

Delphine had always hated cold weather. It regressed her, taking her back to the Depression houseboat where she'd been born on the shores of way-far-south Lake Des Orages. Her father had stuffed newspapers into the cracks to keep the cold out, but it found ways in anyway.

Cold was what they'd made their winter living on. *Cold* is what thickened the furs they trapped and sold.

But she didn't have to love it.

"I sure wish I could go to Bois Sec and see where you live, Mamère," Cam told her as they window-shopped earlier that day while A.P. worked at Maggio's. But with Mickey—unexpectedly—having declined to accompany them, things were seeming a little less merry than they should've.

Cold for Christmas. Still and always.

"Well, boo," Delphine let him pull her along windy Canal Street where tinsel decorations rocked among the streetlights above their heads, "maybe we can do that another time. Don't guess we'll get around to it on this trip."

"Why's Mom acting so weird?"

"I wish I knew."

He stopped in front of Maison Blanche and then dragged her inside when he saw something he liked in the department store's windows. "I need to go in here for a minute. I hope I have enough money…"

"I'll loan you some." She waited.

He purchased something in a white bag, then took it to Gift Wrap, eventually emerging triumphant, a small New Yorker at home in large stores. His large front teeth shone as he held it up to her in all its glittery glory. "For Dad. It's mittens."

She nodded. Then nodded some more, and laughed. "You're what A.P. would call 'very perceptive'."

He trudged along beside her, blowing out his breath in white puffs for their mutual entertainment. "Terry Lanzl calls me *astute*. What does 'astute' mean?"

"I think it means perceptive." She took his hand at an intersection and waited for the light to change.

"You don't need to hold my hand, Mamère—I'm not going to get run over." He tried to shake her off, miffed.

"Here's McDonald's. You too grown up for a Happy Meal?"

His smile was as winning as A.P.'s. "Nope."

"*Mais* you think like your daddy sometimes. Only A.P. would think of buying A.P. some mittens." She pushed open the door and accompanied him past tables full of tourists, high schoolers, families, and the occasional homeless person.

"So Dad is astute?" Cam got in line to order his Happy Meal.

Delphine just shook her head. "He's original."

* * *

Mickey was reading *Time* magazine when they got back to the Marriott room, slumped in a chair in a big terrycloth robe, delicate face unhappy. Neck still rosy from a hot shower, a towel turbaned her wet hair.

"Gotta poop, gotta poop, gotta poop—!" sang Cam.

"Yes," observed his mother, "all this junk food you're craving…"

As he galloped into the bathroom, she turned and crooked a finger at Delphine, whispering, "I've called the airlines. We've got a flight out tomorrow at noon. I never should've come, Delphine. I made a big mistake by coming, I'm sorry."

Delphine's stomach went hollow. Her knees gave out. She flopped down into a green plush wing chair.

"Look," Mickey continued coolly, eyes on the closed door of the bathroom, "I'll handle Cam. Don't know what I'll tell him yet, but I'll think of something. You're the one who's going to have to tell Adrien. Because I don't know what to say to him, and I don't want to hurt his feelings. I certainly don't want to make anything more out of this than it is. But it's just terrible timing, is all."

"Oh *cher.*" It was that detachment of hers that unnerved

103

Delphine most. She took Mickey's hand. "Oh *cher*. Don't do this. Please. *Please please.*"

Mickey shook free. "I feel like a terrible person, but I can't help it. I'm not going to see him again on this trip—"

"Oh *cher*."

"—because I *can't*, Delphine. I *can't*. I just can't."

What words does she think I can use? There's no unhurtful words in French or English I can tell him with! She seized the woman's wrist, brown eyes searching Mickey's blue ones, seeking empathy or comprehension, or merely kindness. "Oh *cher*, you don't have to be nice to him and you don't even have to see him, but *please* just let Cam stay through Christmas. It's so soon—today's Saturday, Christmas Eve's Monday night. *Bébé*, I don't blame you if you hate A.P., I know he's acted like a *maudit* fool. Marriage is a sacrament to Catholics, but y'all two were married by a justice of the peace, maybe he thinks that lets him off on a technicality?—We did try to raise him right..."

"Why does everybody think I *hate* him?" Her nose began to turn pink. Her chin reddened, her eyelids. She made slurpy noises, her white hand fluttering up to her face. "Hell, I wish I knew how to *hate* him, I'd be immune. Tell me how to hate him, and I'll stay."

"Oh *cher*."

"Okay. Look. I don't want to be the Grinch—Cam can stay uptown with y'all tonight, that's fine. He can have Christmas with his dad tonight, after the show. Fine. I don't care how late you let him stay up. But we're leaving tomorrow, Delphine. I can't handle it. I thought I could, but I can't."

"But what if—?"

"*Ssshh*. Here he comes."

* * *

Delphine tried out all kinds of explanations on her way to A.P.'s apartment aboard the bus. People around her were probably noticing her lips moving as she repeated scenarios to herself, rehearsing. *A.P., Mickey's mama has taken sick, and she—No. Mrs. Wickham plays golf and goes to health clubs, she's as healthy as a damn horse.*

A.P., Mickey's had to go back to work sooner than she thought—but no. College professors don't work on Christmas.

Son, Mickey's just got to get back to New York. Don't ask me why. She's just got to go. You know why. Be honest with yourself. I don't know why. But you do.

Yet she had no words ready when she let herself into his overheated apartment. He lay in the exact middle of the bed, still in his jacket. "Watch where you step." He pointed at a place near the wall.

"What'd you break?" Putting down her purse and taking off her coat, she moved in on the soggy problem with a dustpan and sponges.

He looked peculiar. It took him a while to answer. "Bee-Bee threw coffee at the wall. Got into a shouting match with Nelson Ryan…" He jerked a thumb at the wallboard.

"*Coo* Lord. Start a race riot for Christmas."

He stood, and she thought he was going to explain. But he closed his mouth, then rubbed at his face with both hands. "I'm going to take a shower, me. Don't answer the phone. I've got the machine on."

Something's not right here. That Bee-Bee, plus the landlord. "You okay, boo?"

"Yeah. Fine. —If it's Cam and Mickey, though, you can answer it. Just tell them I'll call them right back."

She finished with Bee-Bee's mess while he ran water in the bathroom. *Feel like I'm getting a stomach ulcer.* Cold wind challenged her through cracks around the window and she smelled the marshlands.

"You ready?" He paused in the doorway now with his hair wet, buttoning himself into a nondescript shirt.

"Just got to powder my nose." The mirror in the bathroom was too steamed up to be much help to her. She wiped at it with toilet tissue. "So Bee-Bee's big-shot record man's coming back tonight?"

"*Fuck* Bee-Bee's record man. Hope his fucking legs grow together."

"That's an ugly word, son. Don't use that ugly word to me. I'm on your side."

He just stood there and breathed. Slid an arm around her shoulders, but then let it lie there, resting his chin on the top of her head. As if he'd forgotten how to lift it off.

Helping her on with her coat, gathering up his wallet, keys, cigarettes, lighter, and cane, his hands were shaking as he let them both out of the door and into the dark alley; and Delphine understood that he was either looking forward to something tonight a great deal, or mortally dreading it.

I feel very bad. Something's not right.

So do I tell him about Mickey right now? No. There'll be time for that, after I go get Cam. After the show's over. I'll know when it's time. When it's time, maybe I'll know what to say.

Stomach churning, she watched as Kyle and Lamar helped him unload the van at Tipitina's. They were just about done when she held out her empty hand to A.P., saying, "Give me the keys."

"What?"

"I got to go pick up Cam at the hotel. Let me have the keys, when y'all get everything out."

He slammed up the van's back doors. "But Mick'll bring him, won't she?"

"Mickey's not feeling too good tonight. She's not coming."

"Well. *Shit.* That really sucks..."

"Yes, it does."

"Guess she's got to take care of herself, if she doesn't want no bad cold for Christmas." He dug into his pockets, handing her a clump of metal. "Here."

"So I'll get Cam fed, then we'll both be out front for your first show. You sing good tonight, boo."

"I mean to try."

He remained in the glare of her headlights as she backed out, one hand in the pocket of his jacket, the other on his cane. He waved.

Kyle and Lamar had gone back into the club. Delphine could see their silhouettes deep inside the lighted rectangle of door. Her low beams moved over A.P. He wiped an eye with the heel of his free hand.

I'm getting some bad, bad vibes here.

"You can't kill him," Paul had told her. "He's a human roach. Smash him, poison him, he's just like a roach. Gets up and crawls again. So stop worrying, babe."

But her insides knotted up now.

Are you jealous of him, Paul? You resent all this attention I'm giving him? If you'd had the bad dreams I'm having, love, maybe you'd be helping me. Instead of acting like a maudit *asshole.*

She passed the Bridge Lounge on her way downtown to the Marriott. Then, on impulse, parked the van in a loading zone and ran back up the block and inside the bar for a take-out vodka stinger.

A young ponytailed man tried to pick her up. "Hey, you sweet little teeny thang."

She snorted. "I got ingrown toe-nails older than you."

Yes I do, she thought, as the bartender poured her drink into a plastic go-cup. *I've lived a long time, and I've seen a few things. Even roaches get stepped on, sooner or later. You can kill one with hair spray, if you get enough on him.*

CHAPTER FIFTEEN

He knew that Feen and Cam were in the audience, but he was glad that the stage lights lasered into his eyes too brightly to let him concentrate on the pair of them back there, the child and the little woman like a bird.

A.P.'s composure was a spinning top, something that had to keep doing what it was doing, or fall over on its side and just lie there.

The first show went okay, adequate and uninspired. But he didn't risk going out front afterward.

Because of the bourbon.

* * *

Nobody said a word as he sat backstage on a piano stool now and nursed a drink, one foot sending him into an occasional slow spin while he thought about nothing. Frieda Washington tore up a torch song out front, her strong wounded voice bellowing through the building and causing nearby glassware to vibrate in a tinkling rattle.

His slow pivot continued. Kyle orbited into view. "So what're you doing, Savoie? You know yet?"

"About what?"

"Frieda. You signing?"

"Nope." He propelled himself into another revolution, then realized that Kyle might not know he hadn't been asked to. *None of 'em know that it's not my decision? There's a little shred of pride left me here?* "Well, actually, it looks like I might be getting back together again with my wife. Might have to move back up to New York, if she can't get tenure down here. Things're pretty much up in the air..." *—Which is sort of the truth. That last sentence, at least.*

"Don't think I've ever seen you drink before." Kyle pointed at the bottle.

"Want some?"

"No, I'm cool. —So are they buying your compositions?"

"Nobody's said anything to me about it." More truth. He poured a little more bourbon into his glass, a satisfying amber under the naked light bulbs overhead.

Kyle squatted on the floor by his ankles. "And I'm still in grad school. Psychology, at Tulane. So what do you think I should do?"

"Timing is all." —A shrug.

"What's that supposed to mean?"

"Can't tell you what smart timing is, but here's *couyon* timing: me throwing away my work/study program at Nicholls State, my student deferment for one short year to work offshore and make a shitload of money to marry my girl with—her daddy's idea, he got me the job." A.P. shook his head. "Hot wheels to hell, man—I never once suspected the government could find me that fast. Got sent off to Vietnam and didn't get back together with her for... like... three or four years, not until her daddy'd died. And even then, once we got back together, it was toxic. I loved her and she me, but we'd been poisoned. Timing is all."

"Wow."

I can't go into my personal life here, he thought, picturing Mickey's puffy sad face under cascades of blond hair. Black splotches on the pillow beside his head in the mornings where she had cried herself to sleep and her eyeliner had run. *If we'd just been able to forgive each other.*

"Look, Kyle." A.P. drained his glass. "Maybe it's like this. You watch yourself long enough, *podna*, you'll see what direction you're going in."

Frieda's agent, Coley Sanchez-Wilson, crept around backstage like a horror movie bloodsucker. A.P. watched, mute, as Kyle finally approached the diamond pinky rings in supplication.

Frieda'd completed her first set and sat upright in her feathers and her sequined gown, doing something with her fingers under the dim light bulbs. Needle-point.

Ma'am, A.P. sighed, getting to his feet to go onstage, *there's like a million musicians in the country. I had only three.*

* * *

"My name's Adrien Paul Savoie," he said into the mike, just before his final number, "and I'm from Bois Sec way down Bayou Lafourche, where a few of the old folks still don't speak English. M'father's a marine welder and my *parrain* runs a marina, where I used to work. My uncle had him a band, playing swamp-pop all over South Louisiana, and he let me sit in. One of my *papères* built shrimp boats for a living, the other was a muskrat trapper, musician and handyman. He could play, like, five or six musical instruments, but couldn't read—not just music. He couldn't read anything at all.

"I'm so proud of every single one of them. The people I've had in my life, I'm lucky to've had them, living and dead. One of them was my little brother Nicholas. I know he's in Heaven, because he went through hell down here. I pray he forgives me."

Somebody brought the lights down. Behind him, he could hear Kyle and Lamar whispering to each other, puzzled.

The big room was dark when A.P. looked up again. He could see no faces. "My son and my mother are in the house tonight. It took a big effort for each of 'em to get here, so I want to do something special for them, while I got the opportunity."

Isolated applause. He looked around at the band. "Y'all ain't going to know this one…"

Laskey mumbled back something that no one caught, and

somebody in the audience laughed, uneasy. A.P.'s speech was slurred.

But he positioned the guitar on his knees, thought for a moment while a woman coughed in the dark, and then strummed chords. They brought it all back to him, and he began to pick up the waltz pace, unhurried, unworried. Papère's favorite song came out with no trouble at all: *"Jolie blonde, regardez donc quoi t'as fait / Tu m'as quitte pour t'en aller…"*

But then he paused, after the second verse. Because he was picturing his maternal grandfather and thinking *You hated my guts,* maudit vieux! *Calling me 'bastard', when you called me anything. Used to get drunker'n shit and cuss out Feen for being an unwed mother, even after she was married. Forgiveness was foreign to you. Does that get handed down? Is it foreign to me? Forgiveness?*

Everything lurched to a halt. No-Frills looked at one another.

But you taught me guitar. And I'm drunker'n shit.

A.P. scratched at his cheek. "Hell, I'm drunker'n shit, me!" he amiably announced to the house. "Y'all want to party?"

Affirmative yells rattled the ceiling. Somebody in the audience requested the old Isley Brothers' rave-up *Shout!*, and No-Frills could do it and they did. A girl in sandals and a peasant skirt leaped up between the tables to throw herself at the music, unshaven armpits brown and fuzzy. Frat boys and punks, African-American secretaries and lawyers, nurses and bus drivers of all ethnicities, hippies and golfers and college girls, chefs and oil-field roustabouts collided in the aisles, feet bringing up dirt, dried rice and droplets of muddy spilled beer from the floor.

Hot red stage lights burned A.P.'s shoulders as he raved himself hoarse, shirt soaked, knowing that if he fell into the audience, he would not hit the floor because his listeners were jammed together shoulder to shoulder. They would bear him up. He felt wonderful.

I could die right now. Always leave a party when you're still having a good time. I should fall on my head and break my neck right now before everything goes to hell. Before it's all over.

They were called back at the end of the set for two encores, A.P. and No-Frills, while Frieda Washington and Coley Sanchez-

112

Wilson waited somewhere behind them. A.P. could feel them back there, sucking the life out of him, as he introduced his band members. *Y'all let me have my time. Yours is coming.*

Stumbling backstage after the house lights came back up, he badly needed to be off his feet. He got out of sight of the audience, then sat right down on the floor.

The crowd out front was still yelling his name. He wished he could go back out there now and just sit on his stool and tell them about Cam. About Mickey—*ma jolie blonde. Who I need to forgive.*

Somebody took him by the elbows. *Two* somebodies. Lamar and Kyle. Yeah, he could walk. Yeah, he was drunk...

Coley Sanchez-Wilson had contracts, cigarettes, congratulations and Champagne on ice for everybody. –Well, almost everybody.

But A.P. took a whole open Mumm's from the bucket, set his guitar down against a wall, then sat hunched over in an armchair in a far corner with the bottle between his knees. *I deserve it, and I don't need no glass for it. Like he's offered me one...*

Frieda was beginning her final set. He listened. There were cigarette burns all over the chair's vinyl cushion. He added a few more, trying to melt his initials into the plastic.

Shoes with feet in them materialized on the floor in front of his eyes. He didn't know how long he'd been attempting arson.

Tiny feet in red high-heels. *Definitely not Bee-Bee.*

Feen put a hand to his sweaty hair, right behind his ear. "Good evening," he told her. "Care for Champagne?"

Sanchez-Wilson crossed his line of sight, shoulder to shoulder with Lamar Legendre now. A.P. had difficulty seeing their mouths move, unable to make out their conversation, but Lamar was laughing. *None of my business anyway...*

"What's the matter?" Feen's voice was cool silk.

His hands went up to his face, but the gap where those fingers were gone exposed his left eye just as it began to leak. Concentrating on getting his lips and tongue to work, he cleared his throat. "Feen, you'd better get Cam back to the hotel. It's late. Mick'll be some pissed."

"But—"

"Don't bring him back here right now… I'm kind of loaded… he doesn't need to see me like this. I'll get Bee-Bee to drop me off home."

"But don't you have to put some stuff in the van, boo? What about your equipment?"

"Beeb's already got it loaded. —There's a joke here somewhere, but damn if I can find it…"

Beaded purse dangling against her knees, her face up there above it was all profound love and profounder worry. "*Mais* what happened, son? What's going on?"

"Record deal's gone belly-up. Man's interested in Frieda, not me."

"*Coo* Lord."

"…Timing is all, Feen."

"Yeah. It's time you had a gallon of coffee…"

"*Mais c'est bon*, sober again tomorrow, *je te promets*—just one little slip-up *ici*, nothing permanent. Just one tiny, little… tiny… Good thing Mick couldn't make it tonight." He tried to laugh. "Be deaf with all her bitching…"

"*Mère de Dieu.*"

"But ask her where she wants to go for Christmas. Brennan's? Commander's? Benihana…? Any-fuckin'-where. My pleasure. Her and Cam and me, 'cause I know you'll be in Bois Sec. Maybe we can get down there ourselves, I don't know. Depends on how Pop's feeling about her, and how he's feeling about *me*. But you come dine with us if you can get away. My pleasure. Tell her I'm buying."

Feen reached into her purse and took out the keys to the van, jingling them as if she were going to say something. But then didn't.

A.P. looked back down, searching for cigarettes and his Zippo. Lit one, then peeled the label off the wet green bottle between his knees, fingernail pulling at the foil paper until it folded back upon itself in minute accordion pleats. Lights reflected from the bubbles inside. *I'm what you call 'sloshed', Mick. You'd kill me.*

Too much bubbly in here, in every sense of the word. Guys all bubbly. Fuck.

Too much Mumm's. And it won't be enough.

When he remembered to look back up again, Feen was gone.

* * *

She unlocked the passenger-side door, where Cam climbed in and buckled himself up, Kyle and Lamar shouting good-nights to them both. That *maudit* bejeweled record man stood near them, casually lighting a cigarette for Laskey in the chill.

Cam yawned. Delphine put her head down on the steering wheel for a moment.

"Tired, Mamère?"

"Kinda…"

"Where's Dad?"

"They've got some stuff to do. He'll catch a ride home with Bee-Bee. He asked me to just take you on, since it's getting so late…"

Her grandson yawned again with a hand over his big front teeth and delicate nose. He closed his mouth. She watched as his fingers plucked at the seams of his parka elbows. "Did you know that me and Mom are leaving tomorrow?"

Delphine drove, unhappy. "Yes."

"But Dad doesn't know?"

"Not yet."

Cam turned on the radio and kicked out with his short legs, fretfully. "Not fair! I'll probably be asleep tonight when he gets home!"

She didn't respond.

"What the…?" He sat up straighter, looking out of every window possible at the motels and junk food restaurants out on Highway 90. "This isn't the way to Dad's place, is it? Where are we?"

The van gathered momentum. Delphine clutched the steering wheel and let the Blessed Virgin Mary do the driving.

They've got a word for what we're doing, she reminded Our Lady of The Kidnappers. *You better make me let go of this wheel and let's have a little heart-to-heart...*

Glancing over at Cam, she said, "You told me you wanted to visit Bois Sec, boo. Timing is all."

His eyes goggled. "In the middle of the *night?* Won't Mom be mad?"

"Probably." *She'll probably call the cops, as a matter of fact. I might go to prison.*

Cam watched the Ochsner Hospital whiz past in a blur of flagstaffs and many lighted windows. "But how far away is Bois Sec? What if we're not back in time for Mom and me to catch our flight out tomorrow?"

"So what?"

His mouth opened and shut. Then hung ajar. "Freakin' *awesome!*" He whistled, once the implications had sunk in. "Holy Everything!"

She nodded, then began to hum *Anna Banana.*

Cam sat back with an amazed grin, as the old van rattled over the Mississippi River at the Huey P. Long Bridge crossing and lost itself among the trees and trucks of the West Bank.

Timing was all.

CHAPTER SIXTEEN

Michelle Wickham, PhD., stood on the stoop in the crystalline morning sunlight, pounding at the door of Adrien's apartment while her taxi waited at the curb.

Back in her academic mode again, unvarnished and unglamorous, she regarded her watch. The wood of the door hurt her gloved knuckles. Adrien would certainly be at work by now—his Christmas Sunday schedule. The blue van was gone. Good. "Delphine? Cam? Open up, somebody!"

She'd dawdled over coffee and a cruller in the hotel snackery, watching her morning pass in the clock-face on her wrist until it said nine-thirty. Then blotted her lips, grabbed a cab, and headed uptown with her luggage.

Six blocks away, her stomach had begun to knot up. But no, the van was nowhere to be see outside the shotgun double where Adrien's mailbox was screwed to the wall. *He's pathological but he's prompt*, she'd drawn a sigh of relief, instructing her driver to wait. Yet her stomach wasn't getting the message.

The cruller of death. She belched. And knocked again.

Then tried to smile a noncommittal greeting at a shapeless woman who had come out of the other half of the house and was staring down the alley now at the ruckus, hair in curlers and bathrobe flapping around her ankles in the cold. "You're not Jehovah's Witnesses, are you?""

"Um… No, ma'am."

"Well, just so you know. We're Catholics here."

"That's laudable. Merry Christmas."

"Don't waste no pamphlets on this house…" She squinted and moved off with a last look at Mickey's cowgirl boots and clean, free hair. *I'm probably the first non-Delphine female she's seen in Adrien's vicinity fully clothed.*

The taxi honked. How embarrassing, having to shout in public this way. *My mom would pass out.*

"Hey!" Mickey used less volume, lips right at the wood, "Cam Savoie? I know you're in there, pal—!"

Ear to the door, she heard noises on the other side of it. Subtle crashes. The latch clicked, finally—fumble fumble fumble—and it opened two inches.

In the crack appeared an eye like a cherry tomato. "Hey," croaked a voice. And Mickey's blood pressure went right off the charts, because both eye and voice belonged to the drunken wretch she'd left five years ago. Stale tobacco smoke and sour wine stunk up the air, polluting the morning.

There he swayed in the cracked opening in his underwear, unshaven, coughing. Sounding like a whole cancer ward.

And Cam has to see this, she lamented, dashing back down the alley through the gate to yank her luggage out of the cab, throw a twenty-dollar bill at the driver and abandon her change, running back *up* the alley again to push the door open into Adrien's head with a loud bonk. Clothes were in a wad on the floor. Liquid was spilled in a puddle on top of the round table, dripping off the edge into his Adidas. Cigarette butts lay everywhere like dirty confetti.

She dumped her luggage on the floor.

"Champagne in the fridge, help yourself," he offered, hoarse. "I'm going back to bed…" –Said while collapsing face-down among blankets, beer cans, Champagne bottles and a little canister of prescription meds. His feet didn't quite make it, sticking out over the rusted iron railing at the foot of the mattress.

She hugged her arms close to her body and stood over him like the Spanish Inquisition. "Where's Cam?"

"Cam's with Mickey."

"*Dammit!*" she yelled, throwing her purse to the floor, "*I'm* Mickey!"

"Oh yeah. Quite right. Sorry."

Marching into the kitchen, fury making her neck and jaws ache, she saw no trace of Cam. But marijuana detritus lay all over the table, a plate full of seeds, a little packet of rolling papers and several forlorn roach-butts in a ceramic ash tray stamped *Virginia Is For Lovers*. Mickey felt her arm come swooping down and she didn't try to stop it—she gave it free rein and felt a visceral thrill when it sent all the mess smacking into the walls and *Virginia* came to pieces with its cargo of illegalia.

"What's the matter with you animals over there?" came a man's shout through the wall.

Delphine's roll-away bed stood nearby, folded up. The bathroom was empty. Mickey raised the bathroom window with a lunge, putting her mouth to the screen: "Delphine? Cam? Y'all out there anywhere?"

No answer. Frost glistened on a blasted banana tree.

She closed the window and ran through the rooms. Adrien was out cold. She picked up one of his sneakers and threw it at his head, then wrenched the door open and went sprinting down the alley in her boots. Fleeing through the gate onto the sidewalk, looking up and down Tchoupitoulas Street, confirming what she already knew: *no blue van.*

Frantic, she retraced her steps, screaming "Get off your drunken ass!" while bending down, taking hold of Adrien's ankles, trying to pull him off the bed. "You fucking *bum*, you fucking lunatic *reprobate...!*"

"Seen my pain pills anywhere?" He raised his head.

She let loose a barrage of blows onto his shoulders, fists pounding in unison, desperate. "I'm going to *kill* you—I'll fucking *kill* you—I'm going to *kill* you, you asshole! Where's Cam? *Where's Cam?*"

The child's name ignited some spark of comprehension in him, finally. "Cam? —Ain't he with you?"

"*If he was with me, would I be here yelling like a maniac?*"

Rolling over onto his back, he put a forearm over his eyes to combat the light. "Let's see... I rode home with Beeb last night— you know Bee-Bee? Yeah. And Feen... let's see... Feen took Cam to the Marriott after the show. Yeah."

"Delphine *did not* bring Cam to the Marriott, pal!" Mickey went to the telephone, lifting the receiver with a shaking hand. *Stay calm*, she coached herself while dialing Information. *Just stay calm. You've got to make yourself understood.* "Hello? I'd like the number of a Walter Legendre, please. In Orleans Parish, I guess. —No, I don't know the address, I'm sorry..."

"Where's Cam?" came a croak from the bed.

"*SHUT UP! JUST SHUT UP, ADRIEN!*"

The operator gave her a number and she punched in its digits. A female voice answered on the third ring: "Yeah?"

"I'm Mrs. A.P. Savoie. This is an emergency, ma'am. May I please speak to Mr. Legendre?"

The response was glacial, in both temperature and speed. "He be leaving for work right now..."

"Please. *Please*, ma'am. I've got to speak to him. Can you catch him?" She chewed her lips.

The sun came higher through the dirty window. The phone popped and rustled on the other end, then came a bass voice. "Yeah. Who ziss?"

"Mr. Legendre?" She almost wept. "This is Michelle Wickham. I met you at Tipitina's, night before last. —Michelle *Savoie*, I mean. Mickey. Adrien's wife. Ex-wife. I'm blond, I have a little boy—"

"Yeah, what's up?"

Can't tell if he's irritated, worried, or just bored. "Well, Adrien's mother has disappeared with my son. Adrien's dead drunk—but you knew that. I don't know if there's been a traffic accident, or..." *Don't CRY, you idiot. This isn't a patient man.*

But she heard a muted discussion in the background on the Legendre end. Then: "Where you at, Miz Savoie?"

"At Adrien's. The van is definitely gone. Cam and the van."

"Stay put. I'll call the police, see if there's been any wrecks and so on. Then come by and quiz Savoie. I'll get him woke up."

"That's just so thoughtful…"

" 'Thoughtful' got nothing to do with it—my damn sound board's in the van."

"I'll make up any work time you lose, Mr. Legendre. I'll make it worth your while—"

"Sound board and a microphone worth my while. Kid and his grandmama's probably just gone out for breakfast. Old van could take a hit with a semi and still roll—got seat belts. Or somebody would've left a message on the answer machine there. Light blinking?"

She looked. "No."

"Good. Make me some strong coffee, by the way." He hung up.

Oh God, don't let Cam be hurt. Don't let there be a wreck. Don't let him be scared, or in the hands of evil people. I'll be good and kind and patient with everybody for the rest of my life. With my students. Even my mother.

Her back and shoulders cold, she kept hugging herself. And put the coffee on to drip, then poured herself the first cup. But did not touch it, just sat at the table in front of it and put her head down onto her arms. Listening for rescue.

Adrien lay senseless on the bed. One corner of her eye could see the pale blur that was his uncovered legs. She turned her head away, sedating herself with waiting and the rhythm of her own breathing.

The alley gate clanged.

She found her feet under her of their own volition, carrying her to the door. Then held it open for the man coming through it like a bear. "No wrecks," he announced. "No murders, no shootings, no wrecks."

"Thank God!" Her knees giving out, she sat on the edge of the mattress.

"Now that there," he pointed at Adrien with his cigar, "*that's* a wreck."

Agreeing, she nodded. "Not only alcohol, either... some pain pills, too—don't know how many, but not enough to kill him, apparently. But oh my Lord, what do I do now? I've got a plane to catch at noon..." *Terry's meeting it this evening, and if I'm not on it, he'll go totally Terry. TOTALLY Terry. Especially if the Jets lose today's game.*

"Sure the kid ain't just gone shopping with his grandmama or nothing?"

Getting to her feet, she found her coffee and sipped it. Ice-cold and bitter. "Ahh... they didn't come to my hotel last night at all, that's for sure. And I don't know if they ever showed up here—Adrien's beyond interrogation. But it looks as if Delphine's little bed in the kitchen hasn't even been unfolded..."

"Well," Bee-Bee unzipped his hunting jacket and took off his tweed cap. "Let's get him some sober. Go run me a tubful of cold water."

She ran to the bathroom but did not light the gas heater. Just turned the cold water on full, shuddering with chill and delight. *This promises to be horrible, but it serves him right.*

Then turned off the tap when the water became deepish, calling "Okay!"

Bee-Bee bent grunting with effort, hoisted Adrien's limp form over one massive shoulder, moving carefully so that he wouldn't bang his head into anything. "Pour me a cup of that coffee, Miz Savoie. Squeeze some dishwashing soap in it."

Mickey shuddered again, stooping to go through the few items stored under the sink. "I don't see dish—"

"What's down there?"

"Laundry detergent."

"That be fine. Dump in about two teaspoons."

She complied, thinking *He deserves it* with somewhat less conviction as the mixture foamed evilly.

Bee-Bee stood burdened at the bathroom door, Adrien's dark head dangling at his rear. "Just think you ought to know we lost our band last night, Miz Savoie, him and me. Representative from Hightower Creative Management signed up every single man for Frieda Washington. Except us two."

She blinked twice. Three times. "I had no idea. I'm sorry to hear that."

"I got some drunk myself last night, that's why I be late for work this morning. So I ain't in no mood to lose my sound board and my microphone, too."

"Put me down," Adrien mumbled, a disembodied voice from Bee-Bee's backside. "Got the *mal de coeur*..."

"Don't know what that is." Bee-Bee lumbered heavily past her into the bathroom.

"I think it means 'nausea'," said Mickey, beginning to feel bad. "I think he's about to puke."

"Not on the seat of my pants, you ain't." Then came a splash, a sudden hoarse yelp choked off into gargles, and Bee-Bee calling out, "Bring me the coffee!"

She galloped, hot foamy potion sloshing. Bee-Bee had one hand stuck around the mildewed shower curtain, pressing down on Adrien's streaming forehead, submerging him up to the eyebrows.

Mickey waited. "You're drowning him!"

"No. Getting his attention. Now reach me the cup..." He pinched Adrien's nostrils together, elbowing away two uncoordinated fighting hands, and poured the brown liquid into the mouth opening to gulp breath. "Make him puke his guts out, *mal de* whatever. Throw up any alcohol or pills might still be in his stomach. Better go back out there, Miz Savoie. Big mess coming."

"I've been through it all before."

Adrien choked and began to retch. Bee-Bee hauled him halfway out of the tub, aiming his head over the nearby toilet bowl.

Heaving, he vomited foamy liquid. Mickey crouched and bent over him, cradling his face from behind in both hands to keep his teeth from shattering against the porcelain. "Come on, pal," she muttered, hair in her eyes. "Get it out. Get it all out."

"Now get me a blanket," said Bee-Bee when the vomiting brought up nothing more, and they wrapped him in the dirty dry coverlet. He shivered, violent jerks, blue-lipped.

She watched the big longshoreman toil back into the front

room with him to lay him down on the bed again with surprising gentleness. "Miz Savoie, we need a lot more black coffee…"

Adrien coughed. "Hold the Tide."

"Got to work on kidneys. See can you find me any aspirin or ibuprofen." Bee-Bee looked at Mickey without expression. "Nothing with acetaminophen in it—shut down his liver. Blood sugar's probably all fucked up, too. Some sugar in the coffee might help."

Mickey spoke to Adrien. "How you feel?"

"Y'all just stripped out my stomach lining with phosphates, how the hell you *think* I feel?"

"Well, you got to get up now." Bee-Bee was implacable. "Cleanse the blood. Flush out them kidneys. Walk around, drink that coffee, and piss. Then walk around, drink coffee, and piss some more."

Adrien leaned over the bedside and retched, dry. Nothing would come up. "There's a 9mm Ruger in my closet. Finish me off."

"Stand up. Give me your hand."

He held the blanket closed at his collarbone but let Bee-Bee haul him up onto his feet, one arm slung over the bigger man's shoulders.

"Okay," Bee-Bee told him. "Take this Motrin right here."

"Don't let me go. Whole room is spinning…"

Bee-Bee held on. "Hand him that coffee over there, Miz Savoie."

He tossed back the caplets and the liquid, eyelids down too low for Mickey to see inside. But his condition had ceased to please her. She strode into the kitchen for a coffee refill at his request. "Put a lot of sugar in that next cup, babe, please. I got the shakes."

"I am."

The pacing of the pair had resumed when she returned, Adrien's blanket trailing behind him like a cape, sculpted torso a damaged statue's, Apollo post-Vesuvius. She sat mute on the bed, watching the labored movements of the injured hip and knees, one thigh thinner than the other, genitals heavy in the wet briefs, raw-looking stigmata scarring his belly, the topography of this beautiful broken body as familiar to her as her own. What was unfamiliar now was the shock of it. *He died over there. In that war. With some part of him still un-resurrected, even today. Embracing oblivion.*

"Okay now." Bee-Bee was matching his instructions to Adrien's slow shuffles. "Listen up. Seems your mama done run off with your boy, and my sound equipment. In your van. Where would she go? Lady here's got a plane to catch."

Mickey's frantic, silent *No! No!* went unnoticed. Too late now...

Adrien paused. "Who's got to catch a plane?"

All she could do was lower her head, irritated.

He looked from Bee-Bee to Mickey. "Babe? What day is this? — Shit, did I miss Christmas?"

"You were working on it." She raised her head.

Comprehension dawned across his face. "You're going home early? Running out on me?"

"You care?"

"You weren't even going to tell me?"

"Delphine was supposed to do that."

He rubbed his face with his free hand, the black stubble of beard making an almost audible rasp, then grabbed the blanket to keep it from slipping. "You maybe should've come clean and just *told* me, Mick. Don't involve Feen in *anything*. Not in *anything*. Because this is what happens."

"I... didn't want to be the bad guy." *And I'm not, am I? You're the bad guy. Aren't you?*

He sighed. "Hey, Beeb? Let me go, *podna*—I got to take a leak."

Bee-Bee complied. Adrien had more balance now, and went staggering off to the bathroom, stumbling in the doorway to the kitchen but righting himself before either of them could get to him. He waved.

Bee-Bee looked at Mickey. Shook his head. Then actually smiled.

"Bee-Bee." She spoke his name.

"Mickey." He spoke hers.

They exchanged the deep nod of collaborators.

Oh shit—Terry! She suddenly remembered what day it was. *I need to call Terry. Leave a message on his machine while he's at the Bills game —"Don't come to the airport until I tell you, we might be taking a later flight…"*

From the kitchen came a small crash, then the sound of the refrigerator opening. Mickey stood. "Adrien?"

He materialized in the doorway with a can of beer.

She made a wordless sound, flabbergasted, and then lunged for it. He seemed surprised at her disapproval, holding it high over her head. "No, wait," he said. "I need it, babe. Hair of the dog."

Lumbering footsteps came up behind her as she tried another grab, cigar smoke in her face as one large hand moved past her ear and easily plucked the beer out of Adrien's under-fingered hand. Silently, Bee-Bee stowed it back in the fridge.

"Just one goddam *beer*, Beeb, come on!" And it wasn't a plea, but a challenge—he'd shoved his arm and shoulder into the open door before Bee-Bee could close it again. Sleepy eyes were mild on the bigger man, but they warned. "My house here, *podna*! None of your business…!"

"Missing sound equipment's my business," Bee-Bee announced without rancor. "I'll break your fucking arm. Snap it right in two, here and now. Think I won't?"

Mickey's mouth had been open so long now that her tongue was dry.

Neither man took his eyes off the other. The fridge blew its cold breath out into the room. "Hair of the dog," repeated Adrien. "*One* beer."

"No pain pills, though—Break your fucking arm…"

"No pills. Just one beer, *je te promets*. –I mean, I promise."

Bee-Bee nodded finally, stepping to one side. Adrien reached inside the cool interior, bringing the beer back out, regarding Mickey. "You want a Coke, or something?"

She shook her head in disgust. "You are too much. Just too much."

He toasted her, then drained the contents of the can, finally setting it on the floor between the toes of her boots. She stooped wearily for it and pitched it into the nearby garbage bin. "Listen, Adrien. *Please.* I don't know how much of this has sunk in. Delphine's got Cam. She's got our *baby*, Adrien. Where would she go?"

"I know she's got him, I didn't just fall off a turnip truck! But she ain't no criminal, and she ain't no pervert! Wherever he is, he's okay!"

"But he's not with *me.*" Her face collapsed into itself, mouth drawing up, nose turning red. She put a fist against her cheek, pressing in at her eye. "I'm sorry—I can't help it—he's so little, and I don't know where he is, and he's not with *me*…!"

"Oh, Mick." He reached out to comfort her.

But she turned away from him, sobbing, face mashed against the door jamb. "I'm sorry, Bee-Bee… I'm not a weepy person… but…"

"Mickey. Babe." Helpless, Adrien kept his hands a foot from her body. "I need you to talk on the phone for a minute, and you can't do it if you're crying."

"I've already called Terry. Left a message…" She looked around herself for a Kleenex or something, finding only a grimy dish towel. But wiped her eyes with it.

"Here." Adrien handed her the phone at the end of its long cord. "Disguise your voice."

She stared at him as if he wore a Groucho nose.

"When somebody picks up, ask for Mrs. Savoie. Try not to sound so Texan."

The look she gave him got funnier and funnier, but he dialed the number and handed it back to her. At the other end, the receiver lifted on the third ring. "Is Mrs. Paul Savoie there?" she asked the girl who answered.

"No, ma'am. May I take a message?"

Adrien leaned in closer, whispering, "Man's voice?"

She shook her head.

"Let me have it." He took it from her, putting it to his earring, sitting down near Bee-Bee on the bed. "Hey, Aura? It's me. A.P. Look, is Feen there? No… No… No."

Mickey took his wrist. "Is she—?"

He waved her off. Listening. "Where's Pop, then? Oh. Yeah. – No, she took it… I'll tell you all about it when I get there—it's kind of involved. As soon as I can, I guess. 'Bye."

Bee-Bee lit another cigar as Mickey waited.

Adrien pinched the bridge of his nose, looking around himself as if needing orientation. "Auradele says that a van—mine—is parked outside the house…"

The breath she hadn't known she'd been holding came out in a deep, grateful sigh. "Thank *God*."

"…but they didn't know who'd left it there. They thought Feen was still here in New Orleans. Somebody left the van there in the middle of the night."

"But she's not there?" What he was saying had begun to seep in. "Delphine and Cam are *not there?*"

He took her fidgety hand. "They ain't far. Can't be. But you'd better call the airlines and cancel, babe. And please call the store for me while I'm getting some clothes on, and tell Mike Maggio I'm sick or something. If he fires me, he fires me." He turned. "Hey, Beeb? I hate to ask you this, man, but can I send you to work today in a taxi? I need wheels, and your car—"

"Ain't about to drive *my* car, all drunked up." He flicked cigar ash, putting his tweed cap back on. "I'll drive you."

"*Mais* what about your job? Sunday overtime?"

"Taking a sick day myself. I'm entitled."

Adrien jerked open bureau drawers and the closet door, dressing himself in jeans and multiple layers of shirts under a shapeless pullover sweater with engine-grease stains at the wrists. "You look like a homeless person," Mickey told him as he pulled on two pairs of socks.

He glanced up. "We'll be outside all day, Mick. Feen's took a pirogue. You going to be warm enough in that?"

Outside all day. She regarded her own gray wool skirt and boots, Mexican sweater under a light windbreaker. *Delphine's in a boat.*

"Well," Adrien took up his cane, "if you get cold, babe, maybe you can borrow something of hers when we get to the house. Jeans."

"The fact that I'm nine inches taller might make it difficult..."

"Stuff your ass into something of mine, then."

"Just let me stay dressed," she hedged. "I haven't seen your family in a long time."

"Neither have I." He loaded jeans pockets with wallet and keys, his cigarettes and Zippo lighter hurried into an old camouflage hunting jacket along with other personal items. "*Maudit* head's killing me—you going to let me pack any Motrin?"

The three of them headed out to the rusty green Buick parked under a leafless rain tree, Adrien climbing into the back seat without argument, lying down on it and scrambling around to find a comfortable position. "Mick knows the way out there, Beeb. If y'all could just stop at a Seven-Eleven on the way and get me about six candy bars and some Gatorade, I'd sure appreciate it."

She turned, watching him roll up his jacket for a pillow. "Hey, I'm sorry about No-Frills. I just want you to know that I know about it..."

His eyes closed and hid him.

Bee-Bee pulled away from the curb, turning on the radio—*Oops:* Frieda Washington. Gone in a violent twist of big fingers, as suddenly as she'd come.

CHAPTER SEVENTEEN

C am had been asleep by the time Delphine had turned into the shell-paved road leading off from the highway. Not dawn yet. Clouds hiding moon and stars.

She cut the engine and let the van roll the last few yards into the rutted driveway near her own rose garden. The house was dark. A single yellow bug light shone at the corner of the shed.

Cam's head lolled against the seat back. *Don't wake up*, she thought at him as she silently closed the driver's side door.

Then snuck across the yard.

A dog trotted out from under the house, wagging its tail, sniffing her high heels. She patted its head, climbing the steps to the *galerie*, pulling open the screen door without squeaks. Found the lock and stuck in her key.

The silence in the house was thick enough to cut, except for Paul's snores. Delphine removed her shoes, tiptoeing barefoot through the bedroom door. He never stirred, never even grunted— *hooray for beer*—as she found her way to the armoire by touch and took out a pair of Keds from its bottom. Located what felt like denim, and stacks of folded-up winter clothes atop the footlocker on the floor.

Then stuck a Brown & Root billed cap onto her head, creeping back out, gathering up a flashlight, can opener, and pocket knife from the kitchen drawers on the way. *Paul*—mon bon vieux mari —*don't be too mad at me. I don't know what else to do. To buy some time.*

Cam was still asleep, tender and dear.

The shed out back was locked, but she had a key. She let herself inside, risking the flashlight now, sending its beam searching among shelved motor parts, gill nets, Mason jars, coffee cans full of nails, nuts and bolts, and fish hooks. Tools lay about, and Thermos bottles. Dodging Paul's bass boat parked on its trailer in the middle, she examined the walls and finally took down an automobile battery from its sagging location, an old truck headlight partially wired to it, setting the heavy discovery on the dirt floor at her feet. *Where's my maudit shrimp boots at? Inside the house? Haven't seen them since La Toussaint...* But Bobby's calf-high pair stood by the door—could she make them fit, if she pulled them on over her Keds? *Yes.*

Amassing gear, she slipped the padlock back onto the shed door, then checked on Cam again, his blond hair shining like gold in the yellow light of the single outdoor bulb.

Damn. I've forgot something.

Kicking off the sloppy boots, she risked another trip to the house, but it had to be done. The guns were racked in the living-room over the TV set, and she took down a serviceable rifle in the dark and, against all odds, found ammo by touch in a kitchen drawer.

Thank God I'm not one of those women always re-arranging furniture. Thank God I keep bullets in the kitchen.

Weak-kneed, she escaped back outside and went to the van.

"Cam!" she whispered and shook him. "Wake up now, boo!"

He smacked his perfect lips once, scrubbing at his face with a fist, looking so peaceful and holy that Delphine hated disturbing him. Then his eyes opened. "What is it? Where are we?"

"*Shh*," she warned him with a finger pressed to her mouth, helping him unbuckle his seat belt. "Come on."

He noticed the rifle. "Cheez. Are we on the run?"

"*Mais* yes, and you'll be our running lights, once I get the headlight wired up. Stand right there. Don't go away. Let me get changed." In back of the van, she tugged on jeans and hunting shirts over her lacy underwear while he made the silent acquaintance of a dog or two up front.

At her signal, he followed when she finally shuffled in her white rubber boots to the dock, transformed. "You're a very weird grandmother, I'll say that much."

Stooping, she tried to look into his eyes in the murk. "You unhappy, boo? We can call this off. Right now."

He shook his head no. "It's not Christmas yet. I'm not ready to leave yet."

At a loss, she wadded up her dress in the stern of the pirogue, then loaded in the rifle, extra clothing, and a paddle. There was nothing she wanted more right now than just to take Cam inside the warm house and bed him down on the living-room sofa, then go crawl under the covers next to Paul and slide into sleep. She craved caffeine. She needed appreciation. She felt old.

Really, finally, *old*. Bone-weary, thick-headed, depleted, out of ideas. Defeated, fragile, useless, unwanted, *old*. But someone had to do something. People could drink themselves to death. Her father had. It could be done.

A faint turquoise haze had begun to show in the eastern sky.

Seating Cam in the bow with the headlight, she wired it up to beam their escape route to Somewhere.

CHAPTER EIGHTEEN

"I got pregnant in high school," Mickey confessed to Bee-Bee as he drove them down Louisiana Highway One later that same morning. "Daddy forced me to have an abortion. Adrien's a Catholic, abortion never even crossed his mind. He wanted to marry me."

"I'm one, too." Low sunlight came through the car window on Bee-Bee's side, Bayou Lafouche glinting to the left. "Got mortal sin on the brain?"

"Well, maybe it *was* a sin—I don't think his parents know about it, not even now." She gnawed the stump of her thumbnail. "Maybe God finally gets around to punishing you."

"Listen, Mickey—"

"Oh, I'm not worried, I'm not worried. Cam's definitely with Delphine, so what do I have to be worried about?"

"Yeah. Miz Savoie ain't going to let nothing happen to her grandchild out here. Woman got web feet. All them Coonasses got web feet."

She glanced over the seat's back. Adrien's sneakers didn't seem special.

"Not him," said Bee-Bee. "Reformed Coonass. His little mama, though—she Orthodox."

"But how can she do anything so outright *crazy?*"

"Hell, you somebody's mama yourself. Think about it."

It was a bright and sunny Sunday beyond the car's windows. Mickey thought about it. "Well. Yeah."

"Ain't you done something crazy in your life?"

"I married what's in the back seat."

He made no comment, his face expressionless. The Buick swung into the passing lane without its turn signal, neatly rounding a slow fuel truck. Denuded sugar cane fields stretched in all directions, their crops harvested, the land flat.

"I know you're his friend," said Mickey, "and maybe that was a low blow."

"Nothing 'friendly' about it. Just trying to get my sound equipment…"

"Well, you should've known him when he was young. Before all the shit hit the fan. True-blue, one hundred per cent, one in a million. –Am I making any sense?"

A shrug. "None of my business."

"My parents just about died, when I got pregnant. They loved Adrien in the abstract—hell, *everybody* loved Adrien—but as my boy friend, as a prospective son-in-law, he finished just above Illegal Alien. The abortion broke us up. So when I went off to Tulane, my daddy was tickled to death. Pre-med students at Tulane. Frat boys heading for law school. Guys who played *golf*."

"Hmph." Maybe this was a laugh.

"When I next heard of Adrien… Oh, Bee-Bee. I dreaded seeing him like that."

"Yeah."

"Don't know how much of my dread was guilt or how much was pity. But when I *saw* him, it wasn't guilt or pity. Just whatever it'd been in the beginning. Just… love. He was on crutches with his left hand and leg ruined, but when he looked at me with those eyes, nothing else mattered. All I wanted to do was be in his arms, and that's where I ended up. Oh my God. Love. Love. Love."

"Won't pay the rent."

"No. We lived together, lived apart, lived together again. Finally got married by a JP on MacDougal Street, in New York's Greenwich Village, me pregnant with Cam, Adrien dead drunk. No wedding, no family, no clergy. No frills."

"Yeah."

She had reminded herself. "What about your band?"

"Gone." Bee-Bee had chewed an unlit cigar to brown paste but would not light it, despite her insistent permission. She tried not to look at it now.

"I must've missed something. I thought Adrien was *good.*"

"Yeh, he good."

"I mean, *real* good. Big-time good. The genuine article."

"You catching on." He nodded. "Sanchez-Wilson don't get it. You get it. *I* get it. In the right hands, Savoie could make some money. I don't know whose hands is the right hands, though. Must not be mine."

"Got an IQ over one-forty, and lives like a bum." *And I don't care if you're overhearing any of this, Adrien, because it's the truth. All of it.*

"Well," Bee-Bee sighed. "Wake him up. Sign up here for 'Bois Sec', and I don't know where we're going."

Oh Lord, we're already past the shipyard, way south of the Intracoastal Waterway. I'm not ready for this. Her stomach turned over a time or two. She dug around in her purse for a mirror. "I know where to go. Just drive on through the business district until this highway junctions with one at the bridge. I'll tell you when to turn."

The community itself had changed little, she saw. There were more convenience stores and fast-food outlets now, but the oil bust had left local businesses as shabby as ever. Wide Bayou Lafourche ran down the center of town parallel to the highway, and the shrimp boats and oil-drilling barges and tugs on its surface still astonished with their diversity and high standards of upkeep, float-ing businesses in better shape than the town itself. She gawked—remembering—at the trawler nets high above her head as the car passed. Then cracked the window, the air out here smelling of creosote and fish.

Robin's Lounge—Adrien used to play there with his uncle. The Come On Inn—they were there too, just about every Friday night. Me underage, him also. Nobody bothered about it, people brought their kids.

The high school, however, sported so many new wings and additions that she would've never been able to verify its identity without a sign out front. A traffic light turned red in the distance, and she knew they were nearing the marina. "Take your next left up here, Bee-Bee. Here's Bayou Bois Sec, branching off, and we're going with it..."

The church is ahead of us, Our Lady of Lourdes, but we'll turn before we get there. The graveyard. The tombs.

He complied, the Buick rattling over a drawbridge near the dock where a store fronted gas pumps. "What now?"

Tee-Jean's Tavern—a real rough place, fights breaking out regularly, the bandstand behind chicken wire. Closed now, she saw with regret. *Roof's just about to cave...*

Too bad. I never got in, he wouldn't let me come. Now I never will.

"This road follows the bayou for a while," she told Bee-Bee. "We just stay on it, then turn again..."

"Oooo-*weee!*" He rubbernecked as they passed an incongruously large and well-gardened white house under gigantic ancient oaks, situated way back from the highway on a spacious mowed lot, twin Mercedes in a roomy garage alongside, satellite dishes out back. Stables and a white picket fence surrounded the property, shiny brown horses like statues on the tan winter grass, with a brass sign proclaiming this a National Historic Landmark shielding the front gate. "Shit, what's this here? Dope dealer?"

"Old sugar plantation, way back when. Oil money, now."

He shook his head.

She looked at him, after a moment. "I used to live there. In that house."

"Well, pin a rose on your nose."

Clamshell-covered dirt roads led off in all directions, several paved ones going to God-Knew-Where. Their new street names, new signs, meant nothing to her. Bee-Bee slowed, then pulled over while Mickey thought about it. There were unfamiliar buildings out here, tire businesses, a day-care center and a Wal-Mart—not too many, but enough to disorient. She reached into the back seat and shook a sleeping shoulder. "Wake up, Adrien. We're in Bois Sec."

He sat up slowly, slapping both stubbly cheeks with his hands, looking out of all the windows as if newly landed on Mars.

Mickey waited. "Don't we turn somewhere around here?"

"Yeah," he answered, but with no real sound. Hoarse. "Hang a left up there, Beeb. Right by that sign."

"How you feel?"

"Not good. —Now do a right on that other road, right up there…"

Mickey gripped the dash, the Buick pitching over ruts in the muddy clamshell gravel. She knew where she was, now. And knew what she'd see as soon as the car rounded the next bend and cleared some trees: a cypress house—its sagging *galerie* facing the bayou up front, invisible from back here—squatting beneath aged oleanders and oaks; empty rusted oil drums abandoned in the weeds; boats and pieces of boats overturned on pilings; the hulk of a 1953 truck without axles or doors, parked forever up against a shed, and a rain-barrel here at the house's right rear corner.

How many times Adrien must've thought about this place, she realized. *How many times. Offshore. In Vietnam. In New York City. I've lived everywhere. I used to live just up that highway back there, and I don't feel a thing about it. Adrien didn't even have a home until he was three.*

How will Cam feel about home? Where will home be, for Cam?

With the name, her fear returned like a sudden tsunami: Cam gone, blond-headed little baby gone God-Knows-Where, maybe with a web-footed grandma. Or maybe Grandma's lying in the swamps somewhere, murdered, with Cam in the hands of a perverted kidnapper, you read so much about these things—

The three-pronged touch on her shoulder was Adrien's. Reading her mind. She reached up and squeezed the two fingers and thumb of his bad hand.

"Feen's got him, I promise you," he said. "I promise you, babe."

She nodded, mute.

The Buick rounded the final bend. A dented blue late-model pickup sat under a large oak near the back of the shed, and Bee-Bee applied the brakes.

"Shit. Pop's home." Adrien puffed out his cheeks and blew.

His own van was parked nearby. Bee-Bee pulled in beside it, a chorus of barking dogs heralding his arrival. He cut the engine but did not open the door, not with those slavering mouths on the other side.

"They'll dirty up my skirt," Mickey told Adrien, "if they don't kill me first."

He climbed out with his cane and they were all over him, but drooling and wagging. "*Va-t'en*, Chaney, *va-t'en! Tais-toi*, Tee-Boy, *tais-toi!*"

"Hey!" came a shrill shout from the back door, a clapping of hands. Some woman stood up there in purple slacks, her long thin hand shading her eyes against the sun. "Here, Chaney! Here, Tee-Boy!"

Mickey doubted. "That's not Bay-Bay, is it?"

"That's her." Adrien hugged a dog. "Guess she's a redhead now..."

In a happy frenzy, the dogs raced from him to Bay-Bay and then back again, as she came trotting in their wake across the white clamshell gravel, squealing. Hounds parting, she slammed into her brother with a bear hug. "You *stranger!* You ol' city-boy, you! *Coo Lord*, how long has it been? Let me look at you!"

Mickey reached for the door handle but Bay beat her to it, leaning into the car to embrace her, auburn curls stiff with hair spray. "God*damn*, it's Mickey Wickham, I can't believe it! You look so good, girl, you're breaking some *law*! How you stay so thin? Mama's side of the family is all thin, but look at me, I put on twenty pounds when I had Jason—!"

She wasn't really fat, but she did weigh enough to keep Mickey pinned in one place: "Wait'll you see Aura—now *that's* a little girl starting to turn some heads at—"

"Bay, this is Mr. Walter Legendre, my friend and manager." Adrien took her by the shoulders, pushing her closer to the steering wheel where Bee-Bee sat dumb-founded by her chatter. "Beeb, this is my sister, Gloria Vidrine."

Bee-Bee nodded, speaking around his cigar. "Mornin'."

"Pop's inside, A.P., and he's pretty mad." She stood. "He seen that van first thing when he got up, didn't know whose it was. 'Somebody's just left it here on my property like it's stolen,'—with the pirogue gone, too, he soon noticed. So nobody went to Mass, and he called the sheriff."

"We know where Feen's got to yet?"

"Well, that's mostly why he's mad. He's been upset with Mama for months, A.P. He *stays* upset with Mama. She also took some stuff from the house and the shed last night—that's how he figured out it was her. Too late to keep the sheriff out of it, though, and now he's embarrassed."

He squinted, eyeing the bayou. "Think she went to Nonc Lucien's?"

"Could have. She's got a rifle, a pirogue and some gear—she's so little and strong, she could paddle herself that far, easy."

"Got my little boy, too, that's what she's got."

Her jaw dropped. "*Cam?* Cam's with *Mama?*"

"She's not running away from Pop, she's running away from *me.*" He shoved his hands into the pockets of his hunting jacket. "Trying to keep Mickey in Louisiana so I won't get drunk. Didn't work. Long story."

"Y'all excuse me a minute," Bee-Bee spoke up, "but can I check on my equipment in the van?"

"No keys," said Adrien without moving a muscle. "Feen's got 'em."

Bay turned to Mickey and Bee-Bee. "Well, y'all come on in, *mais* don't take anything personally. Just a man getting old, arthritis in his hands, wife never home anymore to make him a hot Sunday breakfast."

Paul Savoie was at the kitchen table with coffee and the newspaper, sun-browned face flanked by thick gray hair, deep crow's-feet pleating his temples, uncommonly solid-looking. Deliberately staring up at his visitors over reading glasses, dark eyes took their time. His hands were large and square, and Mickey didn't care for the way he gripped his cup as if he meant to crush it.

"*Ça va, Pa-pa?*" Adrien spoke.

"Hey, Pop," Mickey said to the eyes, feeling like an idiot, wiping suddenly-damp palms on the seams of her skirt. "Ahh... Merry Christmas! How've you been?"

"Feen's took our little boy," Adrien waded right on in, "but you had no way to know that. We still don't know where she is—I'm just sorry you got involved. You don't need this. I'm sorry."

"Well, Feen can just go to hell," Pop said finally in a conversational tone, trilling his L's in a thick Lafourchais accent making the words clang like a warning bell. "*You* can go to hell."

Adrien's jaw tightened. He stood motionless, eyes bloodshot, rumpled in mismatched clothes, unshaven, wild hair all on end. Mickey watched him study this warm kitchen with its faded curtains and battered linoleum floor. She followed the track of his sad gaze.

Auradele, washing breakfast dishes, spoke from the kitchen sink. "Let me get y'all a cup of coffee."

"Don't believe I care for none," Bee-Bee muttered, "thanks all the same."

"Pop, this is Mr. Walter Legendre, my friend. Feen made off with some of his stuff, too. We're all in this together."

"You find her," Pop said, "tell her to just keep going."

Silence.

Glass crashed—Auradele had dropped something near the sink or into the sink or under the sink. Mickey mashed the fabric at the pockets of her skirt into wet knots.

Pop turned in his chair to see what his daughter had broken.

"All right," Adrien said to the back of his head, "I didn't expect you to help me. I'll find 'em myself."

He swiveled back around, studying his son for a moment, looking him over from top to bottom, lighting a cigarette and rubbing the side of his lean cheek, laughing. Then took up his reading glasses and went back to his newspaper. "Hell, you can't even find your own ass to wipe."

"Bee-Bee?" Adrien beckoned. "Mick? Y'all come outside and help me with the boat."

Pop's lips barely moved. "Lay one finger on my boat, I'll report it stolen. Try me."

Nothing. Then everything—Adrien suddenly going from zero to sixty, snatching up the phone from a counter, slamming it down onto the table. Its bell jingled, his father's coffee sloshing. "Here. Call the fucking sheriff, Pop. Bet you got his fucking number memorized by now."

Mickey crossed the floor when she heard trouble in him, but he shook her off and hobbled into the living-room to take a gun down from the rack. "I'm stealing a 12-gauge shotgun too, Pop! Come take an inventory!"

Pop rose instantly. "*Arrête!*"

Filling his pockets with shotgun shells, Adrien paused and shrugged. "*Eh bien—parle.*"

"*Je n'ai rien à dire.*"

"*C'est mauvais...*" He shrugged again with just his brows, making for the kitchen, but his father grabbed him by both shoulders and shoved him against the door jamb.

Before either Bee-Bee or Mickey could react, the gun stock smashed down on Pop's booted instep, Adrien butting it into the man's gut the next instant with a soldier's crisp motion, restrained but *terribly* firm. "Beeb?" he finally called out, unblinking. "How much you want your sound equipment?"

"A whole lot of much."

"Then please go break the lock on that shed out there, *podna.* Pop puts me in jail, Feen'll have to make somebody else her mission."

* * *

It took him less than ten minutes to get Pop's bass boat out of the shed, off its trailer, and into the bayou, while Bee-Bee tugged on a pair of waterproof hip boots made for a somewhat smaller man. Mickey expected a deputy to pull up any second now. She stood at the dock, biting her nails.

"But you're not going with us," Adrien told her when she tried to set foot into the blue-and-white fiberglass hull. "Won't be enough room."

Bee-Bee sat in the passenger seat behind the windshield, uneasy, but took up no space aft. "I see lots of room," she said.

"There's a chance we can't go all the way in this though, babe. Might have to switch over to a pirogue when the water gets shallow, if Feen ain't where I hope she's at."

"Then let Bee-Bee stay behind."

The sun was full in his eyes when he squinted up at her from under a Saints baseball cap. "Somebody might have to help me, if I can't make it all the way by water. Can't use no walking cane in the mud, and boots'd just weigh me down. You can *carry* me, Mick?"

"Well—my God—I certainly don't want to stay here and wait for the sheriff!"

"Don't blame you," Bee-Bee told her. "Feel the same way, and I can't swim a lick."

"Don't matter can you swim or not," said Adrien. "Hip boots'll fill up and drown you, Olympic Gold Medal or no..."

Bee-Bee glanced down at the thigh-high rubber footwear he was wearing.

Adrien laughed, a falsetto yipping. "*Mais* it's okay, Beeb, I can't swim now either. And water's no deeper'n dew most of the way, I guarantee you." He pushed the cap back off his forehead a little, then blew on the palms of his reddened, ungloved hands. Shod only in his light-weight Adidas, his cane left behind in Bee-Bee's Buick, he finally squinted back up at Mickey where the wind blew her hair and flapped her windbreaker. "Well, come on, then. Let's see how far we can get."

She stepped down carefully when he offered her a hand, settling herself aft of Bee-Bee, and hugged her arms close to her body.

Adrien saw. "You cold?" he asked over the idling of the engine.

She shook her head no, in a lie.

He slowly steered them away from the dock, careful to make no wake that would intensify erosion of the bank here near the house. But thoroughly opened 'er up further down the channel, the sleek hull cutting the glassy surface like dressmaker's shears. Mickey held her windbreaker closed in the speeding frigid wind and hoped that Cam wasn't cold. Bee-Bee hunkered down behind the windshield, uncommunicative—impossible to even guess what *he* might be thinking.

No more houses, this far downstream. Only bare-limbed cypresses, where the bayou and its banks melted into each other. Bright green waxy-leaved arrowhead plants grew in the margins, warmed and protected by the relative heat of the water. Mickey pointed. "They sell those things in New York..."

Bee-Bee cupped his hands to shout at Adrien, "Hey, Savoie? Want to let's you and me go into the florist business?"

Mickey again heard that sound that she used to hear more of, her husband's high-pitched, artless, boyish laughter. "Got a shovel?"

The corners of her mouth jerked upward. He turned and grinned at her over his shoulder with his white teeth, black Saints cap crammed low over his brow where it would not be blown off, gold earring glinting, looking to her like some kind of modern-day pirate. *He's enjoying this*, she realized. *He's more himself, out here. Even after all this time.*

Full of the salty smell of the nearby Gulf, the air seemed newly balmy—or maybe that was just the heat from the brilliant sun. But she leaned back, giving her hair to the wind, and remembered this sea-scent, young Adrien Savoie seated cross-legged on the dock with her, guitar on his knees, singing songs of water and storms, summer, and love.

Maybe I'm more myself out here, too.

She thought about Christmas in Manhattan, what she was missing at this very moment. *The rush to buy the best brie in Bloomie's gourmet department, Terry and me fighting shoppers over taxis on a day like this, arms laden with dry white wines. Mama in her mink with Aunt Lillian up from Houston, both of them bitching about the dirt, crime, and high prices. Cam looking out of our apartment windows, down at unhappy pedestrians trying to navigate through traffic and banks of grimy, sooty snow...*

145

Dear God, I ain't nothing but a Texas gal and the Gulf blows its winds over my old homeplace.

* * *

Mickey had no idea where she was, but homeowners here had sunk wrecked old cars into the water to combat levee erosion. Tall Chevron signs and utility poles in back of the houses and trees testified to relatively higher ground, close to a highway. Two Lafitte-skiff commercial fishing boats chugged their way past the posted signs requesting "No Wake".

Adrien made for a dock at the mowed levee in front of a well-kept, beige aluminum-sided frame house next to a matching garage. The boat idled in, slow and tentative.

"Are they here?" Mickey touched his shoulder. "Delphine and Cam?"

"Maybe..." He seemed to be looking for a clue, scanning the waterline. "Feen's brother lives here. She could've got here by pirogue, easy. –Hey, Beeb? Can you give us a hand, please?"

Bee-Bee squirmed up onto the dock, tied up the boat at Adrien's direction, then pulled Mickey out. They both hauled Adrien up onto the gray wood.

"Y'all stay here a minute, and let me go talk to 'em," he lit a cigarette and started up the dock to the house. "My aunt's one of them women never ready for company, lives in a bathrobe twenty-four hours a day..."

Bee-Bee sat down on the dock, re-lit his cigar and circled his knees with his arms, squinting his good eye against the sun. It was definitely getting warmer, sunny with a wood-smoke snap to the air. Mickey saw smoke coming from several chimneys, but not from the one in front of them. She watched Adrien's back as he toiled across the muddy lawn.

Bee-Bee stowed away his matches. "Where we at?"

"God knows." Her eyes stayed on Adrien, who leaned into the doorbell button up there, holding it in for what seemed like five minutes. He finally pulled open the screen door and knocked.

Bee-Bee watched. "What's he got?"

Adrien was studying a scrap of paper he'd snatched out of the lock. Then wadded it up, threw it off the porch, and kicked the door twice in sudden savagery.

"Nervous breakdown?" Bee-Bee struggled to his feet.

That second kick did indeed unbalance him—Adrien lost his footing and went down on hands and knees in a twist that brought both Bee-Bee and Mickey galloping from the dock and up the porch steps.

He can cuss in Vietnamese, she remembered, and maybe that's what he was doing now, because she couldn't understand a word of this hoarse tirade he made right at her cowgirl boots, and not all of it was French.

She looked down. "Delphine's not here, I take it."

He rested his forehead on the wooden floor, Saints cap askew. "Nobody home—they're probably at Mass. She left 'em a real nice note, though: 'I've borrowed your boat. Merry Christmas.'"

She crouched, "Sit up, pal. It's all right."

"It *ain't* all right, I'm sorry, babe. —Shit, we're *all* going to fucking jail..."

But a weight had fallen from her. She took deep, clean, thankful breaths now. *'Merry Christmas"—Delphine would've never written anything so chipper, if Cam were in any kind of trouble. 'Merry Christmas': what gorgeous words!*

Her hand rubbed over Adrien's shoulders. "Sit up, baby. They can't be far. You've gotten us this close."

He sighed, maneuvering what was the worse of two bad legs out from under him, sitting up. Fumbling for a smoke, weary, watching the air in front of him. Then pocketed the Zippo. "Babe," he finally mumbled around the cigarette, "Feen ain't just gone to a neighbor's, you understand."

Mickey rocked back on her heels for a moment. "So where would she go? What's out here?"

His fine, long-nosed profile exhaled blue smoke. "Lake Des Orages... Little Lake... The marsh..."

Bee-Bee crouched. "Camping? Fishing?"

Adrien brushed black curls back with both hands, sticking his cap onto his head. "Hell, y'all, her daddy was a *trapper*. Had him a houseboat and leased acreage in the marsh around Lake Des Orages, they stayed out there all winter, him and his kids. Probably still tie up out there for recreational purposes—goddammit, Feen! —*pic-kee-tôi*, all you *couyon* Robichauxs! Wish each and every *maudit* fucking one of you was sunk ten miles in hell! *Voilà merde!*"

The day became less sunny. Mickey squinted. "So what're you saying?"

"I'm saying you better prepare to stay at the Marriott for a long, long time." He shrugged her off and went limping back across the lawn to the dock.

She ran after him, boot heels sinking in mud. "So that's *it?* We just give up, and go back to New Orleans?"

He passed the moored boat, searching the tall weeds at the bank until he discovered a bottom-side-up pirogue hidden under the dock, and began to drag it out into the light. "Never said that. Y'all two can do what you want."

Bee-Bee immediately caught on to what needed doing and helped him haul the little craft onto and then over the side of the dock where it ended up piggyback inside the larger boat, Mickey looking from man to man.

The Robichaux garage had no windows and was padlocked. Adrien eyed it, straightening the cap on his head. "Think you can break the latch off another door, Beeb?"

"Hope y'all come see me when I'm in Angola Prison." Bee-Bee put his weight to the wood. Hardware groaned, the padlock bracket pulling away.

The interior smelled of petrochemicals and mildew. Adrien examined its dark interior, dodging a few Styrofoam funeral wreaths—faded—that stood incongruously against the walls with a humming deep-freezer. "Feen's got keys here," he handed a paddle and a pole out to Bee-Bee. "Drives over and checks on stuff, whenever my aunt and uncle go to Branson..."

Mickey shook her head, following him back to the dock. "But if there're hundreds of squadillions of miles of shoreline around Lake Des Orages, how——?"

"Think I'll be able to remember a few." He took the shotgun from the boat. "Used to go out there with her all the time…"

"Yeah. And you were only two or three years old."

He jerked at her sleeve, pointing at the open garage. "Here's where I leave you, babe. Might have to travel by pirogue, eventually. Not enough room for you. –You'll be warm enough in there?"

She looked in. Observed some aluminum lawn chairs folded against a deep-freezer—she'd be able to sit. *But this isn't a good idea. The Robichauxs'll return and have a fit…*

But Adrien was already scribbling words on the back of a folded blank check taken from his wallet, turning it over again to finally write "Void" across its front in a diagonal slant. "Here. My name and address is printed on it. I wrote 'This is my wife, Michelle. Our son is missing, she'll tell you all about it. The shotgun is collateral for all I've taken.' "

"I just *stay* here? What if somebody attacks me, or something?"

He handed her the 12-gauge shotgun, showing her how to use it. "You can shoot anybody you want to. Just blow 'em away, I don't care. Keep it against your shoulder, or it'll knock you down."

"But—"

"Babe, you want Cam back this year or not? Yes or no?"

"Don't *patronize* me! I'm about thirty seconds from a psychotic episode as it is!"

He nodded. "I've had better days myself, me…"

She unfolded one of the dusty lawn chairs, sinking wearily into the faded plastic webbing with the weapon on her lap, letting her arms dangle over the sides, stretching out her booted feet. "But I'm calling the state police on her, if you're not back by dark, Adrien. Going next door if I have to, and asking to use the phone…"

"Just do whatever you think you've got to do." He pulled a paperbacked Tom Clancy thriller out of a roomy pocket of his hunting jacket. "Okay, here's something to read. Pretend you're on the subway."

"Thanks. But this *is* kidnapping, Adrien."

He nodded. Turned. "Bee-Bee? Going or staying?"

"Broke into property belong to some white man?"

"Okay. Let's roll."

She watched them through the half-open garage door as they loaded paddle and pole into the little pirogue in the bigger boat, Adrien looking back once at her, waving.

His engine started and then chuffed away.

She tried to read. The air coming through the half-open door was chilly, yet she needed the light. And wanted to be able to see out. *Tom Clancy. Okay, why not?*

But a premonition began to settle upon her, uninvited, that she'd never see Adrien again. —A dumb notion, one of those scare-bombs going off in an anxious mind for no reason at all, but she couldn't ditch it and it rattled her. Like a Tom Clancy plot, a thriller, Adrien just leaving like that with no warm send-off from her, not even a thank-you...

It sent her to her feet, finally. To the door, where a shaft of sunlight came through.

I love you, pal, she told him, suddenly terrified. *Always have. Always will.*

I love you. I love you. I love you.

CHAPTER NINETEEN

He waited until he was well out of Mickey's sight, before taking the flask out of a jacket pocket and unscrewing the cap, keeping one hand on the wheel, risking a backward toss of his head. Then he held it out to Bee-Bee.

Bee-Bee declined, flexing his arms like they felt stiff, frowning vociferously as if he needed to strangle somebody with them to get some relief. *Probably me.*

A.P. put away the whiskey and gunned the boat down the channel. Marsh grasses buzzed by. White birds waded far off. The land out here was as flat and low as the water itself, monotonous, all one color in all directions: all brown, all weedy, all sunlit and cold.

They emerged from what was now only a thready waterway into an inlet, then the inlet became Lake Des Orages—bright and gray as steel, with foggy margins. And further off, no margins at all, just blue sky meeting flat metallic water. A small motorboat with two people in it was the only craft nearby, a man and woman casting from anchorage. A.P. passed them fifty yards to their starboard side and waved.

"Who they?" Bee-Bee wanted to know.

He shrugged. Keeping to the southeast side of the lake, patient with his speed until they were in deeper water. The engine didn't sound right. There was a definite change in RPM, maybe weeds in the propeller. The hull slammed rackety-rackety-rackety over the wake of a passing inboard job with "Painted Lady" lettered on her transom, a metal tackle box by Bee-Bee's foot clanking and clanging in response.

A.P. cut across a forty-five degree arc of the lake, still making for the southeast, watching inlets and tributary waterways opening up to his vision and then closing again in the grasses. Far-off clumps of dark green trees heaped together ahead like clouds, standing in drier places where live oaks could survive. *Chenieres. Papère used to tie up on high ground...*

He slackened his speed, allowing the engine to idle down into a muffled chug-chug, sidling over to the lake's shoreline and keeping his eyes on his depth finder.

Bee-Bee had been silent for what seemed like days.

"I don't want any lectures," A.P. reminded him.

"My mouth open?"

Gulls circled endless flat grasslands. Most of the trees had disappeared out here and the horizon stretched unbroken, punctuated only by an occasional rotting stump and those distant *chenieres.* The tiny waterways here felt right, but the depth finder indicated no clearance as A.P. sought an entrance. The hull scraped mud. *"Putain!"* he muttered, stopping. Reversing, until he had an adequate depth under him again. The boat rocked from side to side in its freedom.

He tried it again, at two more little channels where their currents—feeding the lake—were nearly invisible, but with the same results. Water too shallow. *Fucking head's killing me. Nauseated as hell...* Killing the engine, quieting the world, he booted out the anchor.

He half-stood to heave the pirogue over the gunwale with a furious scrape, nearly sweeping Bee-Bee overboard with it. The little craft landed wallowing in the channel entrance alongside the larger vessel like something just born, A.P. making sure the pole and paddle were still in it. "Okay, Beeb—Plan B."

"Yeah, and anybody steal your daddy's boat...?"

"Somebody already has: me. –Look, you won't be implicated, I was armed with a shotgun, I forced you into this, okay?"

"Yassuh, Mistah Over-seer, sah…" Sullen, Bee-Bee climbed carefully over the side of the bass boat into the narrow little pirogue, keeping it close with one hand while A.P. did a butt-scoot over the gunwale and clambered aboard. He pushed off with the pole from the weedy black mud, the blue-and-white hull of Pop's vessel appearing desirably large and accommodating now as it receded. *No leg room in a pirogue.* Seated in the stern with his feet under him, he took up the paddle.

They glided smoothly over brown shallows, A.P. digging into the water first on one side and then the other with strong, J-shaped strokes, the grasses almost too high to see over on both sides of the channel. Bee-Bee finally looked back, watching for a while. "Anybody ever call you 'asshole'?"

"*Mais* yeah. Mickey. All the time."

"Where we at?"

He shrugged. "The marsh. Water out here's brackish, that's how come the trees get sparse. Used to be more of them out here, before the salt came in from the Gulf so much."

"What's out here?"

"Ducks. Muskrat. Nutria. Fish. Alligators. Oysters. Shrimp over there in the lake…"

"Let me ask a stupid question: You know where you going?"

A.P. looked out over the grasses, squinting. "My grandfather used to tie up near here. Feen's took a boat and a .22 rifle. She ain't headed for no Holiday Inn."

"But you know where to go?"

"Used to come out here with her all the time, when I was a little kid. Old man'd throw oyster shells at me when he was drunk. But when he was relatively sober, he'd teach me guitar."

Bee-Bee's determined frown pushed at his eyepatch. He enunciated as carefully as if he were speaking to an idiot, "Do-you-know-where-we-are-*at*, asshole?"

"Well, not at the moment. No."

He turned around, his broad backside once more presenting itself. He was obviously pissed.

There was no comfortable position for A.P.'s bad hip and spine. He shifted his weight, rocking the craft, and lost his momentum.

Bee-Bee looked back when the pirogue rocked again. "What's up?"

"Muscle cramp... *oo-yee-yi!*... gimme a sec." He had to grimace.

For the first time all day, Bee-Bee's face wore something besides a scowl. "Can I—? What should I—?"

A.P. grabbed at his lower back, letting the paddle fall into the hull, trying to straighten out legs and spine where there was no place to do it, leaning out over the stern to become as linear as he could make himself, hissing "Shit! *Oo-yee-yi,* aww my God... oh shit! *Shit!*" through clenched teeth.

Bee-Bee stuck his thigh-high hip boots out over both sides of the pirogue, planting his feet into the mud of the shallow waterway's bottom for balance, then stood, straddling the craft, and bulldozed A.P. into a face-down position with no-argument hands, pulling the bad left leg backwards and upwards into an arched-back angle. Pushing until A.P.'s heel nearly touched his head. Joints popped. A.P. flailed, holding onto the sides of the stern as if he could make fingerprints in it. Blowing, like Mickey in Lamaze childbirth. His Saints cap fell off and floated away.

Bee-Bee held him like that.

"Jesus—some kind of gay porn flick, hope nobody's watching," A.P. wheezed after a moment.

"Tell me when it eases off..."

"It's easing off... it's easing off..." Sweat ran into his eyes. "Jesus, where'd you learn to do this, man? Can I buy you a Rolex?"

Bee-Bee lowering his leg, A.P. could finally turn over and sit up. Bee-Bee sat back down on his own narrow bench, lifting his feet off the waterway bottom, water puddling in the hull. "Don't think them doctors put you back together just right, partner..."

"Well. I didn't give them much to work with." The wind in his sweaty hair was cold. Bareheaded now, he squinted against the light. The wind whooshed in the grasses.

I got no earthly idea where I am.

The sun had started to lower. A small, red, oil-company helicopter whacked-whacked-whacked overhead. Bee-Bee glanced up at it. "So when we signaling for mayday?"

A.P. tried to orient himself, convinced by the sun that he was in the correct quadrant of the lake. *Chenieres* showed their green oaks above the grasses in the distance—no time to search all that. No doubt Feen had accessed the marsh via a deeper channel than the ones he'd found, maybe getting all the way to her hide-out under engine power. *Got a big head start, she could be on high ground even further off than what I can see from here. It'll take literally days to search by pirogue, unless I can figure out where to look.*

He visualized himself at age three, in the bow of one with Feen paddling in the stern, autumn days when the little black gnats bit the hell out of them, going out to make more peace offerings of liquor and cigarettes to an old drunk who refused to be appeased. A.P. had never enjoyed the trip, paying minimum attention to the voyage itself, dreading the half-cracked vituperation that would be heaped upon him and his mother at the end of it.

"Savoie?"

He leaned on his paddle, took out his flask, and unscrewed the cap.

Bee-Bee watched him take a long pull. "I ain't enjoying this…"

"Neither am I."

"So maybe we ought to just give it up, and get on back. Must be two o'clock by now. Your wife's calling the state police at dark."

A.P. shook his head. "Got to find Cam…"

"He okay. Don't your mama know how to treat kids?"

"She's a *pro*. –The Old Lady Who Lived in A Fucking Shoe."

"Shit, you getting drunk again? Well, head on the fuck *back*, if that's the case! Quit making me want to *knife* you, man!"

"Head back?" He sucked his lip. "Hell, you know where 'back' *is*, Beeb? Because I sure don't. –Have a drink."

It was sort of gratifying to see the wide brown face do a

double-take, those big hands going helpless on the gunwales of the narrow little boat. Time coming to a full stop the way it always did whenever A.P. could get a buzz going. So it felt okay, being lost.

Bee-Bee's features displayed disbelief, consternation, and then outrage. And maybe *rage*-rage, but that was okay too. A.P. offered him the whiskey again.

He put the flask to his lips, disgusted. "Some Coonass *you* are."

"State police'll just have to come find all of us," A.P. lit a smoke, studying the *chenieres* on the horizon. "That's high ground, kind of like little islands in the marsh. Mounds of oyster shells the Indians heaped up as garbage a long, long time ago. We can make for one and at least get a fire going, and spend the night there. I won't let you starve or be cold, Beeb, I promise."

"Done lost faith in your Coonassedness."

"So you got a pocket knife on you?"

Bee-Bee checked the contents of his hunting jacket. "Yep. Got only one cigar left, too, and I don't see no grocery stores…"

A.P. took up the paddle again. "I can't do nothing about smokes. But we got oysters—see 'em?—over there under the water. Got a little whiskey, too. We'll be dining like tourists on Bourbon Street, *podna*, I guarantee you." He felt good, even with the hangover, at having time stop this way. "We got my lighter, and your matches. Hell—you can even *steam* your oysters!"

Bee-Bee settled his tweed cap more squarely upon his head. "*Shit.*"

"Yes *sir*—eat all them oysters, Walter Legendre, go back home and jump your wife's bones and make sexual *history*, man…!"

"You think it's funny when you fuck something up?"

I could take him. He's bigger'n me, but I'm younger. He don't like the water. I could bat him right over the side with this paddle, and have him down before he could even yell.

Bee-Bee helped himself to another drink. "Don't mess with me…"

The helicopter noisily passed overhead again—civilian aircraft, but still. A.P. toyed with the sound of it in his mind, that windblown dopplered chopping. Wishing briefly that Bee-Bee had seen something of those Asian rice paddies, that Bee-Bee knew something of the landscape of his past.

The sun was getting lower, the sky clouding up. The air seemed warmer than it had earlier, but still chilly above the spiky grasses where they stood in the water like the rice of a place where it never got really cold, except in the highlands, and then just rain-forest cool.

We grow rice here around Eunice and Crowley, he reminded himself just before the gunfire.

—And then heard it from high ground on his left, knowing instantly that it was small-bore and pacific. But his reminiscing gut did not make those fine distinctions, reflexes overriding his brain and forcing a deep flinch, his mind shouting *No no no, you* couyon pote-sac—*!*

"*Merde!*" yelped his mouth as the pirogue tipped, the brackish channel coming for him in slow motion.

Bee-Bee stuck his hip-booted legs over the side to land upright, but A.P. couldn't straighten his own fast enough. He saw every ripple, every floating mote as he tried to right himself like a falling cat. The first thing to hit the water was the flat of his hand.

He had one thought as he went in head-first: *That was Feen.*

CHAPTER TWENTY

I t was a soft bumping that she heard first. Maybe a crow at the eaves of the houseboat cabin. Maybe her brother Lucien.

"Lucien?" she said to the air, turning down the volume on the boom box near her elbow.

Cam sat in the middle of the floor near the kerosene heater with his dinner of fresh black drum and canned snap beans. Charcoal still smouldered in the grill on deck, where the mallard she'd shot for supper lay ready out there for plucking. Delphine stood, crossing the small warm cabin for the rifle.

The little boy reacted to the click, her wedding ring striking gun-metal. "What is it?"

"Probably some bird."

She stepped to the door and undid the latch. Cracked it open just enough to poke the rifle barrel out. There'd been recent incidents reported on the news programs, bad blood between city sportsmen who spent weekends in the wetlands and the locals who worked the marsh for a living. *Guess which side I'm on?*

Yet there could be no duck-hunting oil executives for miles around, and she knew it. Because they made noise.

"Come on, like you own the world!" she urged one to appear now, the grandson of one sitting on the floor behind her with a fish fillet. She laughed softly.

Cloudy sunlight sparkled in the roots of marsh grass and there was nothing to see on this side. White gulls flew high over. The water was like sequins.

Clunk—another bumping sound.

Followed by a scraping from the port side of the houseboat, its vibrations racing along the deck under her feet. She stepped outside, rifle half-butted into her shoulder, then ran around the cabin.

"Hey!" Cam shouted behind her.

Men were boarding the houseboat, muddy hands on the low gunwales like they owned it.

"*Freeze!*" she ordered, aiming at the smaller of the two—who not only did not freeze, but continued to drag himself on deck with the aid of his companion. It took Delphine a moment to recognize Bee-Bee Legendre, and took even longer for her to realize it was her own son A.P. in her sights.

She lowered the barrel. His hair, clothes, and sneakers were wet and muddy, his breath a white cloud on the air.

"Don't say a thing," he warned her, hoarse, struggling to his feet.

"You're going to get pneumonia…"

"*Tais-toi, tais-toi!*" One hand waved at her in dismissal. "*Ne dis rien.* I don't want to hear it."

She blundered back into the cabin, past a startled Cam, who was at the door and looking outside now, his hands full of fish. Leaning the rifle against the wall, she snatched up those extra flannel shirts she'd brought with her from home.

"I caught a fish, Dad," said Cam in a low voice.

"Yeah. Good." He took the garments from Delphine without speaking to her, peeling off his wet clothes, a sodden pack of cigarettes and a Zippo lighter falling to the deck. Then flung the soggy wad of clothing against the marine-plywood wall in a furious whiplash, where it stuck plastered there for a moment before falling with a sucking *plop*.

"Are you mad?" Cam asked him.

"Just freezing to death…" He jerked on a dry shirt over his

bare torso, fumbling with the buttons. His fingers would not flex. Delphine stepped over to help him, but he turned his back. "Get your gear, son."

Delphine sidled past Bee-Bee, through the cabin's open door. Greasy knives still lay on the counter, dirty dishes and half-empty canned goods, the bag of charcoal still sitting on the floor. "You found us pretty quick, boo..."

A.P., pulling on multiple shirts, followed. "Who else'd be hunting ducks with a twenty-two?"

"Well, just let me wash up a few—"

"*Goddammit, Feen!*" His strong hand snatched her wrist out of the air, jerked it upwards, and almost hurt her. "Mickey's going to call the state troopers on you, don't you understand that? *Leave it! Leave it!*" –almost whistling the words at her, they came out with so little air. He jerked her wrist with each syllable until she bobbed up and down like a cork.

Stunned, she found her cap when he let her go. Then locked the padlock on the open charcoal and dirty knives and canned vegetables, thoroughly flustered.

"Open it back up! Feen!" he was shouting at her again, gathering up his wet clothes and lighter, and Cam's fishing tackle. "You've left the *maudit* heater lit, you'll burn the place up! *Où sommes-nous? Ce bateau est à qui?*"

Her head hurt. "*Ton nonc Lucien*—"

"Pop's calling cops, and Mickey's calling cops, and Lucien'll probably call whatever fucking cops nobody else has called yet..."

"*Ton nonc Lucien*—"

"Beeb? Please go turn off that heater in there, man, woman's going to commit arson on top of everything else! Somebody get the rifle!" A.P. clapped his hands twice. "*Move it*, people! Let's go! Let's go!"

He seized Cam's arm and walked him toward Lucien's bass boat, alongside which Delphine had docked, taking the crumbly fish out of the child's fingers and pitching it into the lapping water. Cam's face went all slack.

"*Mère de Dieu!*" Delphine cried. "Don't take it out on the child!"

He clawed at his mud-stiff hair. "You know how much trouble we're in? You got *any idea?*"

Cam's face was moist like a rose.

A.P. stooped and put both hands on his son's shoulders, helpless. "Cam. Look. I'm proud you caught a fish, and I know it was a big one. But I've stolen a boat. Committed burglary—no kidding. Your mom is worrying herself into a *maudit* coma and she's going to call the law. Somebody'll probably get mad enough to press charges. You dig?"

He nodded.

"Good man." A.P. patted his shoulder. Stood awkwardly. "Bee-Bee?"

"Yo!" He was already in the stern of Lucien's boat and he held out his arms for Cam, settling the little boy into a seat while A.P. dragged the pirogue up onto the high ground beneath the live oaks and left it there, bottom-side-up. The sun was low now, red above the marsh grasses. In its light, Cam's hair was the color of a new penny.

A.P. blew out white breath, surrendering finally to Delphine. "You drive. I don't know where that deep channel is."

"You okay?"

He hoisted himself up onto his hands, coming over the side into the boat head-first. "I've left Pop's boat near that inlet where Bay got stung by the stingray that time..."

Delphine touched him. "Boo..."

He flopped down into the seat next to hers, elbows on the wet knees of his jeans, and she got the engine started. As she pulled away from the gray-painted houseboat in the failing sun and found the deep waterway, he never looked up.

I did it all for you, dearest son, she thought at him. *Surely you know that, my child. You'd have done it for Cam.*

They came out into the lake, south of the inlet A.P. had mentioned, and she decided to make one sweep up the western shore before giving up on Paul's boat for the night. Bay-Bay had caught a stingray somewhere around here many years ago on a family fishing outing, pulling it into the boat over Paul's objections, and had gotten her hands blistered trying to cut the line. They'd had to take her to the emergency room, when it was all said and done. Nobody had ever pulled another stingray aboard a Savoie boat. That had been someplace around here. *Some little inlet where the current into the lake was fairly strong and the redfish were biting. Somewhere. Right around…*

Blue-and-white flashed at the corner of her left eye and she cut the wheel, heeling to port in the shallows, raising a big wake that went crashing up into a small waterway and rocked Paul's anchored boat where it sat. *"Hey hey!"* she exulted, passing it in her momentum.

A.P. retrieved keys out of his soaked jeans and then went over the side into thigh-deep water, Delphine's wake still slapping at his hip pockets as he disappeared into the grasses. Then his head and shoulders became visible. He had climbed aboard and was hauling in the anchor.

"Chez Lucien?" She shouted at him. *"Make for Lucien's?"*

He nodded. His engine caught.

She revved and then opened up, heading for the northwest where the sun lay like a tomato among scrambled eggs. The lake was dark gunmetal now, quiet. The wind had died. She had to take off her cap or lose it in the wind of her speed, though. The engine sounded like an F-16. Nobody could talk. Nobody wanted to.

She glanced back a time or two to make sure A.P. was following. Something was wrong with his propeller.

It'll take months to smooth all of this out with him, she realized. *Maybe forever.*

* * *

Mickey's bright head was a soft beacon in the dusk. Delphine saw it crowning the dark figure at the end of the nearing dock. She heard —over the idling of the engine—cowgirl boots pacing back and forth, punishing the wood.

She didn't wait to see the face. She leaned over the side while the face was still dim and tied up the boat with her reddened hands.

Cam's feet drifted disembodied over her head, as Mickey lifted him out and then knelt with her skirted knees on the splintery boards, his round head tucked under her chin. "Thank God we named you 'Cameron'," she was muttering, shaky. "So many Jasons and Troys and Joshes and Adams your age, but only one Cameron, pal..."

Delphine shoved her hands into the pockets of her baggy hunting jacket. Bee-Bee took the rifle out of the boat.

"I caught a fish. —You're *smushing* me, Mom."

"...only one *Cam*, pal. Only one precious Cam."

She's not yelling at me. Unnoticed, Delphine dragged fishing tackle and rods-and-reels back into the garage. *That means she'll wait and yell at A.P.*

"Where's Adrien?" Mickey looked from Delphine to Bee-Bee.

An engine whined from down the bayou, nearing. Bee-Bee pointed. "He coming. Propeller's fouled and he don't want to push it."

Mickey stood, holding Cam against her thighs, hair wrecked, face shiny with the wind and hours. She breathed deeply, noisily.

A.P.'s motor idled closer; he was coming in in near darkness. The noise stopped, and his silhouette appeared on the water, active. They could hear him throwing objects around, moving tackle boxes. Mickey went back inside the garage and brought out a flashlight, carrying it down the dock to the tied-up craft just as A.P. stood up in the hull and sat on the edge of the wooden planking, swinging his feet up and over and out. Her flashlight took him in.

"Good God!" she said. "What happened to you?"

He just shook his head. "Y'all get aboard here, Mick. I need to go get something..."

She gave him her hand, helping him stand. "My God, you're all wet! You know what hypothermia is, pal?"

He waved her off, Bee-Bee helping Cam into Paul's boat, then Mickey. Who waited, agitated, watching A.P. limp down the dock and through the doorway of the garage. "He's going to catch pneumonia..."

Cam squirmed, restive. Bee-Bee looked at Delphine.

Mickey sighed. "What's he looking for? The shotgun?"

"*What're you looking for, Dad?*" shrilled Cam in his high treble.

"Hush, hush!" Mickey put two fingers over his lips.

Delphine heard something clatter inside the garage. It was dark up there. She hustled herself back up onto the dock and ran clumsily across the yard in her shrimp boots. A.P located the light switch just as she made the open door, flooding the interior with sudden brightness that hurt.

He had already moved several cardboard cartons in the darkness. Hands on hips, he stood near the light switch, looking like hell, mud in his stubbly day-old beard, his hair caked with it.

"What're you looking for, boo? Shotgun's there near the chair."

"Shit," he said, hoarse. "They got that deep freeze in here. No fridge."

"Whole world's a fridge," she observed, "outside."

"You got keys to the house?"

"No."

"*Goddammit.*" He closed his eyes very slowly and then opened them again, even slower. "God. Damn. It."

"What's the matter? Why you need to get in the house?"

"...It's Miller Time."

She stood there in her white rubber boots. Her face twitched. "You mean you're just going to let Cam and Mickey and Bee-Bee sit out there in the cold, while you hunt for *beer?*"

He didn't move.

"So what you want me to tell 'em? I got to tell 'em *something*, son." Defeated tears beginning to spill over, she didn't try to hide them—she couldn't. Here was utter helplessness, at last. She was helpless. "Oh, oh, oh, you're killing me, *mon fis! Mon cher fis!* You're killing me, boo! Please don't kill me! Stop killing things! Stop killing yourself!"

He stirred, finally. Lurched over to the wall and hit the light switch, bringing blackness. Her eyes tried to adjust. She could hear him breathing. "Go on back down there, then," he told her. "I'll be along in a minute."

"*Mais*, you're going to just stand here in the dark?"

"No. I got the *mal de coeur*, real nauseated. Bad hangover. Lost my flask when I fell in. So just get back down there with them. Tell 'em I'm coming, as soon as I can stop retching."

Feel sorta nauseated myself, going back home to Paul tonight, she thought.

Coo Lord, and I'm too tired to fight.

CHAPTER TWENTY-ONE

Paul emerged from the house onto the *galerie* while they were tying up, underdressed in shirt sleeves, smoking and silent. Delphine trudged up the dock and across the yard and up her own steps, coming into the light of the kitchen, finally. He followed, favoring one leg. She put down her gear, looking at his foot. "What happened to you? Been kicking the furniture?"

"Don't start in on me, Feen."

There were suitcases on the floor under the table. Coo *Lord, Christmas already*. She sighed. "Who all's here?"

"Bay-Bay, Huey and the kids. They at Shoney's for supper."

Auradele stood near the sink and Delphine noticed her face change when A.P. came limping through the door, Mickey and Cam right behind him. Bee-Bee had elected to stay outside with his last cigar, near his still-incarcerated sound equipment.

Paul would not look at A.P. "I'm sorry, but I don't want him in here, Feen."

"Well." A.P. held out his maimed hand palm-up to Delphine, after a moment. "He don't want me in here. Give me the keys to the van and let me get these people back to New Orleans, then. It's getting late."

Drained, she went to locate her purse. She couldn't recall where she'd left it, and it took her a while, Paul's aggressive silence sucking all the air from the room.

"Hey, Papère," Cam ventured.

His face softened. "Hey yourself, *tee-boug*. Good to see you, son."

Delphine discovered Motrin in her purse and tucked two caplets into A.P.'s hand alongside the set of keys. He washed them down with sugared coffee from the stove, while Mickey and Cam sat in stupefaction, Cam on Mickey's lap and his eyes sleepy. Mickey looked at nothing, face pink with windburn, her hair in cowlicks.

Paul escaped into the living-room to turn on the TV set full-blast, to what sounded like the Mormon Tabernacle Choir performing *Hark, The Herald Angels Sing* at a volume loud enough to shatter glass. Delphine and Auradele sliced ham and cheese for hurried sandwiches, packing them in Zip-lock bags, stepping around each other in intricate choreography.

"I don't want him in here!" Paul bellowed, unseen.

Delphine put the grocery sack full of food into Mickey's hands, along with a thermos of coffee. "Here's something for the road, *cher*. I made enough for Bee-Bee, too. Give him some."

"I don't want him in—!"

"*PUTAIN! AM I DEAF?*" she screamed back at the living-room, veins standing out on her neck. "I'm packing 'em some supper! Ain't going to send them off from here without some *maudit* supper!"

A.P. was jingling the keys, meaningfully. Mickey stood, Cam asleep in her arms now, his head on her shoulder. Delphine approached her and tried to give her a hug, but it was hard to do while she held the child. "Tuesday's Christmas Day. Y'all going to try to come back out here?"

Mickey just looked at A.P.

"Don't see how we can." He nodded at the living-room, its impossible TV noise. "These two'll probably be back up in New York by then, anyway..."

Delphine sighed. "Yeah."

He bent to kiss her cheek. "*Joyeux Noël,* and thanks for the food. I'll call you tomorrow, let you know what's going on."

"Are you going to be okay, Delphine?" Mickey spoke up.

"What?"

Her eyes cut back to the living-room, and Paul. "You going to be okay, with him?"

Why wouldn't I be okay? "*Mais* yes, I'll just have to listen to him belly-ache for a few hours, is all. Y'all call me…"

"I will," said A.P.

"Drive careful, boo."

He patted her shoulder.

"What century can I get my sound equipment in?" Bee-Bee's head appeared through the door.

Delphine watched them leave, too tired for emotion. She would later be unable to remember whether A.P. had waved to her, or not.

* * *

The van followed Bee-Bee's taillights until Adrien had to turn off onto State Street back in New Orleans. His horn honked Bee-Bee a loud good-night.

Cam had waked up enough during the trip to eat half of a ham sandwich but was out cold on the carpet in back by the time they pulled up to the curb in front of Adrien's apartment.

Mickey carried him through the gate and down the alley, waiting for Adrien to get the door unlocked, and Cam sighed a few times but never stirred. It was cold inside the apartment. Adrien hit the light switch, put his cane in a corner, and lit the heater, while Mickey sank down on the bed with her burden. The red light on the telephone answering machine was blinking.

He went into the kitchen, and she heard the aluminum rattle of the little bed unfolding. His muddy face reappeared at the crack of the door, him crooking a finger at her. Stepping around her own suitcase, she passed through and put Cam down into the soft, small mattress there by the stove, pulling up the covers to his dear ears, finally kissing his cheek while her eyes teared up.

Water splashed in the bathroom sink. Adrien scrubbed quietly at his face and hair.

She was in her nightgown when he came back into the front room, closing the kitchen door behind him. "Will he be warm enough in there?"

He nodded. "I lit the bathroom heater and left the door open."

"Any more of those sandwiches left?"

He handed her the paper sack and she retrieved Cam's leftovers while he cleared away all the cigarette butts and empty Champagne bottles and beer cans from the furniture. Then changed the sheets on the bed, wadding up the dirty ones and kicking them under the Christmas tree, stripping down to his briefs.

"You want any more of this?" She held out the sandwich.

He shook his head no.

She licked her fingers, went to him, and they held each other for a long time. Not saying anything, not doing anything, just standing there locked belly-to-belly and breast-to-breast. The blue flame in the heater sputtered.

Maybe he thought she was beyond making love, because she certainly thought that of him. They turned out the lights, then got under the covers, comfortable with their own body heat. Adrien was not a snorer but he did make sounds in his sleep, fragments of words, the cracking of finger or toe joints as he jerked around in early-slumber dreams. Mickey had none. She fell directly into oblivion.

Her eyes opened again when he rolled over into her, discovering her, waking. His unshaven face was like sandpaper. His erection prodded at her belly.

"Well, hello!" she whispered to it.

Reflections of the heater's flickering light shone from his eyes. His smile was something she felt with her hands.

She pulled her nightgown up and over her head, so they were skin-to-skin when he kissed her. The brine of marsh water and his own clean sweat salted him at neck and groin. His tongue opened her. She was already wet. They were in no hurry.

They made slow, juicy love in the blue light of the gas heater, her legs wrapped around his damaged hips, her mouth on his, silent. Her orgasm was leisurely and lasting.

The answering machine's red light blinked off and on.

When the discomfort from his injuries became unbearable, he put her on top, pulling her pelvis down onto him, letting her take her time. The contours of his face were beautiful, his neck where it met his strong shoulders.

She began to buck, rising up on him like a goddess.

I keep falling in and out of love, she thought, *like it's cyclical. Nine times out of ten, it's with* you, *pal. This same sweet you. So which is real, the falling in or the falling out? Because I'm doing it again, I'm falling in love again...*

He came like a runaway fire hose. She drained him of every drop.

"I can't live without you," he said when he could speak.

"You're doing it."

"This isn't living."

CHAPTER TWENTY-TWO

The room was full of light when she woke, his side of the bed empty. The gas heater glowed steadily. Mickey fetched her nightgown from the floor and sat for a while on the edge of the mattress, in the comfort of warmth and the comfort of comfort.

One of his shirts would make a good bed jacket. She took the last clean one out of his closet and buttoned it over her nightgown, humming *Jingle Bells*.

He was making breakfast when she opened the kitchen door onto savory home aromas of coffee and sausage, his back to her, hair shower-damp and curling. Cam sat at the table munching buttered toast and could not greet her, mouth full, until he had swallowed. But was antic, crumbs on his lips, body language ecstatic.

"Mom's up!" he announced when he could.

Adrien turned. "Pull up a chair, Mom." His voice was still hoarse, but he was clean-shaven.

She crossed the floor instead, wrapping her arms right around him from behind. Minuscule droplets of hot oil popped out of the skillet and stung her forearms. "OOO*ooo!*"

"Hey," he deadpanned, "not in front of the kay-eye-dee..."

"The kay-eye-dee can *spell* now, pal."

"Oh."

They shared an awkward, sloppy kiss over his shoulder.

"You guys know what tonight is?" Cam started up as they got a little tongue into it. "You guys know what happens tonight? Santa Claus comes tonight!"

"Yeah." Mickey put her smile right against the back of Adrien's neck.

"Santa *Dad*, I mean," Cam amended.

"Santa Dad came last night, son," said Adrien.

"Like a neutron bomb," she whispered to his collar.

He indicated the cabinets above the sink. "Get yourself a plate down, babe."

She didn't usually eat breakfast, but she was ravenous this morning. Cam happily scooted over and made room for her at the table, Adrien dishing up grits and eggs and sausage—about the only selections he was any good at cooking, besides seafood. Remembering how she took her coffee, he brought her a cup.

Sunlight poured through the window onto the battered kitchen furniture, and he turned on the radio. Elvis, crooning *Blue Christmas*, Adrien singing harmony as he filled his own plate.

"You have to work today?" she asked him.

He shrugged. Sat down. "Don't know. I'm probably fired..."

"Not for calling in sick, I wouldn't think." She looked closely at him. His color was good. "So how do you feel?"

"Better."

"Let's go to the zoo!" said Cam. "See the white alligators!"

"Time you hit the showers, son," Adrien told him. "Finish your breakfast, then go take your bath."

Cam furrowed his grits. "Dirty kids can go to zoos."

"People could grow petunias in what's under your chin, pal." Mickey drained her coffee cup. "We could package you for fertilizer..."

Adrien stretched and yawned. "Mom's right. If you're done eating, get in the bathroom. No clean you, no zoo."

Cam jumped up, threw down his fork, and disappeared.

Adrien broke into his easy goofy laughter, lighting a cigarette, sticking a bare foot into Mickey's lap under the table.

She stroked its sole. "You up for the zoo? All that walking?"

"Take me back, Mick." His laughter stopped.

"I don't know if we should discuss that right now." She grew immediately defensive, pulling at a strand of blond hair. "We're having such a pleasant morning…"

"So when can we discuss it?"

"Okay, look…" She abandoned his foot. Brought both of her hands up above the table top, laying them flat on it as she stood. "Getting into all this right now is *your* idea, remember—But, Adrien, what hurt me so much is not what you *did*. I realize that love and sex don't always equal the same thing, from a masculine perspective. Men have sex with… with… *watermelons*. With *sheep*. Love has nothing to do with that. I get it."

He removed his foot from her lap.

"I mean," she went on, "I know you've had a hard time, I can understand your over-compensating. You never chose to be an addict. And you've got this inferiority complex about your disability, I know that. Maybe about some other things, too."

"Kick me again, babe," he muttered. "I'm still breathing."

She stacked the empty plates. "I just expected more out of you. You were so self-aware when we were kids, I guess I expected you to just figure it all out and *rise above* everything. It broke my heart, that you wouldn't let me be *enough* for you, Adrien. Enough woman, enough friend, enough reason to stay home and stay sober. You broke my fucking heart."

"…I'm sorry."

"We've got a son to raise. I want him to understand that he has *choices* about his own behavior. About drugs. And girls. And drunk driving." *How much of this is sinking in?* she wondered. *Your face is unreadable.* "If you want to get really white-trash about it, pal, all Cam stands to learn from you is that one twat's just as good as another, don't matter none whose it is. So I'm just a twat. And not always your first choice in twats, either."

"Babe." His voice was almost gone. "I *am* white trash."

"So what makes you think you'd be any different this time?"

"Fear. Of losing you again. I'm so *maudit* sick of losing."

"Would you be faithful to me? Do you even know how?"

He flung his arms up, his hands out. "Mick, I'd jump through hoops for you! Look at what all we went through yesterday, our little adventure! Doesn't that say something to you? Who did I do that for?"

"Cam, mostly."

"*Mais* yeah, of course. But he wasn't in no danger, so come on! Get real."

"So would you go back to AA for me?"

"Babe, I'd sew my goddam mouth shut for you, honest to God!" His big dark eyes pleaded. "Mick, I'd take a fucking bullet for you."

"Oh bloody hell." She tried to laugh. "Maybe if I could just *believe* some of this—"

Cam came galloping out of the bathroom with a crashing of its door, wrapped in a towel around his waist and a cloud of hot steam. "Okay, it's Zoo Time!"

Adrien poked a finger into his bare tummy. "Son, you don't come to somebody's table dressed like a Sumo wrestler. Go get your clothes on."

"We need to find a laundromat and get some laundry done," Mickey realized. "Running low on clean clothes. I'm wearing your last clean shirt."

"Cigarettes." Adrien nodded. "Motrin…"

Cam pattered barefoot through the kitchen to the luggage in the front room, giggling, unzipping his backpack. Mickey got another cup of coffee, then set the cup back down on the table so that she could pull Adrien's head back against her stomach and muss his thick hair with both hands. "What'm I going to do with you, my love? Is it a Karma problem? Are you my bad Karma?"

"Mom?" Cam came back into the kitchen, half-dressed in jeans, his voice a little weird. "Terry's outside."

She didn't understand.

"*Terry*," he repeated. "He's on the steps. Outside. I can see him."

"Terry who? Terry *Lanzl*?"

Cam nodded. "He's getting ready to knock on the door. And he *saw* me, Mom. He knows we're here."

CHAPTER TWENTY-THREE

"Okay if I leave my rental car out front?" Terry asked over coffee.

"Sure. Just don't block the Ryans' driveway," A.P. jerked a thumb at that side of the house.

"Who?"

"Landlords," said Mickey. "The other half of the duplex."

"Warm it up for you?" A.P. held the coffee pot over Terry's half-empty cup.

"No, no." He put a hand to the mug's top. "I'm fine. Had a lot of coffee on the plane. But thanks."

He was making himself agreeable, and seemed like a nice-enough guy. A.P. hadn't wanted to like him, but found himself impressed with his amiability. And his concern for Mickey's welfare. This relative youth of his, though, had come as a surprise. Nobody had told A.P. that Terry Lanzl would be so young.

In fact, nobody's told me anything at all about this person. I don't know jack-shit about him.

Except he's upset. He's hiding it well, but he's sorta seriously pissed off.

"We should've called you, Terry," A.P. apologized again. "It's my fault. My answering machine. I saw the light blinking."

"No," said Terry, elbows on the table, shaking his head. "I

knew it was late, I knew you people were probably somewhere. I shouldn't have just barged in on you like this."

Mickey spoke. "Terry…"

"I mean, I guess I just freaked. —Bad day yesterday, my team lost the final game of the season and now I've lost my job."

A.P. whistled and his brows went up. "*Putain!* Must be contagious."

"So when I called the Marriott, and they said you'd already checked out…" His eyes traveled to Mickey at the doorway, standing there barefoot in her nightgown and A.P.'s last clean shirt.

He's already counted the beds in here, A.P. noticed. *He keeps looking at the roll-away. Trying to figure out just who slept in the roll-away.*

"We're sorry," said Mickey. "I called you yesterday morning to keep you from worrying. Doesn't look like it did any good."

"You said you weren't taking *that* flight, Michelle. You didn't say anything about totally disappearing."

She sighed. "Well, things were so crazy here, you wouldn't believe."

He was still studying her attire, A.P. saw. Considering the shirt —an innocent concession to modesty, or badge of ownership?

Well, shit, it's none of his business! She's still married to me! No court of law in the land could find fault with her being here, in a nightgown, or no gown, or even just a black leather garter-belt!

Okay, I appreciate the fact he's shook over Cam getting kidnapped. Lot of us got shook over that. But it's still pretty goddam couyon *to just hop a* maudit *plane and come on down…!*

"I had a devil of a time finding this place." Terry turned to A.P. now, smiling slightly, swinging his khaki knees out from under the table so that he could hunker over with his elbows on them. "You have any idea just how many Savoies there are in the New Orleans phone book?"

"I'm listed."

"Yes, but only under your initials. I wasn't familiar with your initials. All I've ever heard Michelle call you is 'Adrien'."

"Well," she blew her short bangs out of her face, "it's been a true comedy of errors. But now it's time we try to plan Christmas,

180

because I don't want to ruin Christmas for Cam. —Last call for coffee, Terry?"

"No, thanks."

She padded over to the sink and poured out the remainder, making deliberate noise while she was doing it. *Just like Feen.* A.P. had to smile.

Cam watched TV in the front room, Mickey's banging and clanging drowning out the sound of PBS programming.

"Well, anyway," Terry went on as if he hadn't heard her request at all, "when I got Michelle's call yesterday and was able to finally match the phone number to a Savoie address on Tchoupitoulas Street—well, *bingo*. Christ, I got lost so many times. Kid a while ago kept saying, 'Down by the river', so I drove all the way to the end of—what was it? Broadway?"

"Sorry," said A.P again. *Wish I could record that word and just punch a button: "Sorry." "Sorry." "Sorry."* "I'll reimburse you for your plane ticket. And your trouble."

"*Blsssh.*" He waved away the offer with a hand. "Listen, man, I've inconvenienced you enough as it is. Turns out, I had all these frequent-flyer miles coming to me, anyway. Trip last month to Miami put me over the top again." He turned in his seat. "Michelle? You remember that, baby? Me saying that the Miami trip put me over the top again?"

She nodded, scrubbing the grits pot.

"I really shouldn't be here," he repeated, "but I just got crazy. You know how it is, when you get real anxious? Real agitated? And can't stand the waiting?"

The TV had grown louder in increments.

"*Cam!*" Mickey shouted. "Turn it down!"

"What?"

"There are people next door, trying to mind their own business in peace! Turn it down!" There was an edge to her voice.

"I'm staying at the Pontchartrain," Terry said without having been asked. "The breakfast was disappointing, after all I've heard about it."

Mickey dried off her hands with a paper towel, then swiveled.

"Look, Terry, I don't know what kind of dumb-ass idea you had in mind, coming down here like this on Christmas Eve. But my son has been through a lot, these past few days. And *I've* been through a lot. And if you'd just sat tight—like a normal person—somebody would've called you. Did you think I wouldn't call?"

He shook his head, elbows still on knees. His forearms were freckled, curly coppery hairs covering them. "I didn't know what to think, quite frankly."

"Well, I refuse to have Cam's Christmas all ballsed up, because you couldn't wait a few hours to hear from somebody."

She sure isn't happy. But maybe I'm glad to know mine isn't the only ass she chews.

Terry raised his eyes to A.P.'s. Mournful pale ones, almost as light as a Siberian husky's, shaded by stubby lashes the color of wheat. His thinning hair was strawberry. "Sorry about this, A.P."

"'S'okay."

"I love her. I love your son, too. Does that make you my enemy?"

"Means you got good taste, *podna*."

"Why does she smell like patchouli?"

Mickey crooked a finger at him. "Come into the bathroom with me. Right now. I want a private word with you."

He uncoiled long legs, and stood. There was a New York Jets logo over the left breast of his pullover golf shirt.

Mickey's eyes searched out A.P.'s and met them for a second, but he could read no meaning into the glance. She disappeared into the bathroom with her lover, and closed the door.

Because that's what he was. Her lover. Terry'd had those large hands of his all over her, and had fucked her, and knew how she sounded when she came.

A.P. wondered about the size of his *bibitte*, and his stamina, and the fact that he could literally sweep her off her feet and carry her anywhere she liked. Terry could dance with her. Throw her over his shoulder, like a cave man. *I can't dance good with her anymore. I might can still throw her, but wouldn't she have a conniption if I tried? He's a gym rat and he's paying for muscle, but doesn't he have enough to suit him? To suit her?*

Oh shit, is she scared of him? he wondered with sudden clarity.

"Dad?" Cam stood in the doorway. "What's going on? Where's Mom?"

A.P. pointed. "In the john. Having a conference."

"Terry should just go back home."

"I imagine," A.P. regarded the closed door, "all three of you'll be flying back up to New York together. Today or tomorrow."

"*Noooo!* Tomorrow's Christmas Day! Airlines aren't open on Christmas Day!"

"Yeah, they are, son."

"Not fair! I want to stay with *you* for Christmas, Dad!" Cam wrapped both arms around his father's neck where he sat.

"Don't push your mom, son. She'll do what she can."

"I heard that." Mickey opened the door.

"I didn't say anything derogatory..."

She came all the way out. "I didn't say you did. —Look, guys, I'm going to get dressed, then go to the Pontchartrain Hotel with Terry. He and I are going to settle all this. In private. If it takes all day."

Cam looped his arm around A.P.s shoulders. "So can I stay here?"

"That's the plan."

She looked down at A.P. where he sat motionless at the table, and held out an open hand. He took it after a moment. Her touch was cold, her palm sweaty. "I'll call you," she said. "Okay?"

Don't go. "Okay."

"Adrien, I don't want *you* to pull a Terry and think I won't call, then go messing around the Pontchartrain looking for me. I've had enough of that stuff for one day, pal. Understand?"

"Ain't my style."

She squeezed his fingers, her face trying to say something, trying to reassure him. *Don't go, babe,* he told her with his eyes. *I don't know Terry Lanzl. I don't know how you really feel about him, Mickey. But I think you're scared.*

All he could do now was return the pressure of her hand, though, and she left him like that.

CHAPTER TWENTY-FOUR

A.P. studied his watch by the light of the Christmas tree, and it was eleven P.M., and she still hadn't called.

Cam lay pressed against him like a sandbag, asleep, breath audible in the stillness. Christmas Eve—a very silent night. Few cars passed, up there at the front of the house, out there in the street. He listened for one to slow down, to pull up at the curb and stop, but none did.

It had been a long day of waiting, of watching TV with Cam, of ordering out for pizza. Of opening presents. "Wonderful mittens," he'd told his son, taking them out of their wrapping paper, trying them on. Bright red. But still. "Something I can sure use, *tee-boug*. Thanks!"

So did the football appeal to the child? The video games?

He'd spoken to Feen, briefly: "We'll probably just stay put here, for tomorrow. —Look, I'm expecting a call from Mickey, can't keep the line tied up… I love you…"

And he'd tried to keep Cam awake a little longer, telling him ghost stories so that he'd be too scared to go right to sleep so soon. He wanted his boy's conscious company. *I'm about to jump out of my skin.*

Mick's not deluded enough to permanently pair up with Terry, but that doesn't mean she'll take me back. I treated her like shit. She'll always make more money than me. I'm a nobody, I've lost my band. Hell, I've probably even lost my job at Maggio's.

And—drunk or rehabbed—I'll be in a wheelchair before I'm fifty.

He lay with his arm around his son, wondering how things had come to this pass. How his wife should be down St. Charles Avenue, in another man's hotel room.

On Christmas Eve.

How on earth did I let this happen? What was I doing, all those years I had her, and just kept on thinking everything was all about me? My *disappointment?* My *resentment?*

Dear God, please bring her back to me, and I'll get my ass in Confession before the next sundown, that's a promise. Bring her back, God, and I'll raise this child here like I was raising little Jesus himself. Make AA my second home. Mentally dress all other women in nun's habits.

But he'd made many promises to God before, like the time he was in the Veteran's Hospital, and hadn't kept any of them. Because God had kept none of his.

You let Tee-Nick die.

Cam was awake. A.P. felt him stir. And Cam spoke. "Dad?"

"Yeah?"

"You crying?"

"…Just got the sniffles, is all… Coming down with a cold, from getting all wet yesterday…"

The child shifted position in the light of the Christmas tree, putting a tender and sticky warm palm to A.P.'s face. He paused. "You're lying, Dad."

Mais yes, I am. I'm *lying. Making miserable noises now, and I can't do a damn thing about it.*

Cam held him. "It's okay," he said. "Mom cries, too."

* * *

She showed up at eight the next morning, Christmas Day, in the same clothes she'd worn the day before.

It was Cam who let her in, because A.P. was just finishing his morning ablutions in the bathroom. Daubs of shaving cream were still under his ear lobes when he heard the alley door swing open, then heard it close. Cowgirl boots paced the hardwood floor and his pulse rate went up, like a kid's.

Toweling off his face, he pulled on yesterday's shirt and pushed the door open into the cooler, drier air of the kitchen. Mickey stood there in sunglasses.

"Thought I heard somebody come in," he said, unaccountably nervous. He wanted to go to her but wasn't sure he should. "Where's Cam?"

"Out front. Saying goodbye to Terry." She sounded tired. Like she hadn't slept much.

"Terry dropping you off?"

She sat. Brushed both hands up through her short, clean silky hair. "He's flying back up in a little while. Wanted to say goodbye to Cam, though. And give him his Christmas present."

'Flying back up"—thank you, Jesus! "So how'd it go?"

She sighed. "Nothing's settled. I've convinced him to go home, but nothing's settled beyond that."

He poured coffee for her. "What're you settling?"

"The implications of why I wouldn't sleep with him last night." She smiled as she accepted the cup. "Thanks."

"Cam wearing his parka out there? Because it's cold…"

"I don't know," she said. "I don't remember."

Sunlight through the window lit her face. Her left cheek was purple, high up under the lens of her sunglasses.

"*Hey.*" He put out his good hand for a touch.

She flinched. "Don't."

Gently, he pushed up her sunglasses. Discovering a black eye, a real shiner. Almost swollen shut.

His blood pressure reached the stratosphere. "*Oo-yee-yi!*"

"…I fell."

"*Shit!*"

"It's nothing."

"He still out there?" He grabbed his cane from the corner. "*Pote-sac* still out there, in front of my house, talking to my son?"

"Adrien…"

"I hope he's still out there, because I want a word with him."

Mickey stood. "Don't. *Please* don't. Just drop it."

He wrenched open the alley door, stepping out onto the tiny stoop, barefoot. The concrete was cold, but he didn't mind. He felt very hot.

"Don't make it worse," she pleaded behind him. "*Please* don't make it worse than it already is! I have to be able to get along with him, Adrien. I live in the same city as him. *Please.*"

But his rage was like a conveyor belt, and it conveyed him down the alley to the gate, making his gait smoother than usual, greasing his joints. The gate clanged against the fence as he went through it.

Cam was out front, leaning into the window of a rented Maserati coupe, turning his head when he saw A.P. coming and stepping back a pace. His breath was white in the cold air, but nowhere near as white or thick as his father's.

A.P. stuck his good hand through the driver's side window, yanked on the lock, then wrenched the door open.

Terry Lanzl sat behind the wheel like a lump of dough.

"Come inside for a moment," A.P. told him. "I want a word with you."

"Well, I'd really like to," said Terry, stupefied, "but my flight leaves in about forty-five minutes, so I don't know if I have the time. Could we do this over the phone?"

A.P. reached in, plucked the car keys out of the ignition, then pocketed them. "You're good at booking flights, *pote-sac*, you just book yourself another one."

"What's going on? What'd I do?"

"Assault and battery, looks like to me."

Terry climbed out of the car, miming perplexity. "I told her it was an accident, I never meant to do it. She got in the way, is all. Honestly."

A.P. put a hand to his back. "Let's get inside where it's warm."

They climbed the steps to the stoop, Cam trailing, Terry shaking his head from side to side. "Look—it was an accident, I was punching furniture. And she said, 'Don't do that,' and tried to stop me. You can ask her. She just got in the way. She's a volatile lady—you know that. Knows exactly how to push my buttons."

"What she pushes is between you and her." A.P. opened the door for him. "But you physically push her back, that's between you and *me*."

Mickey had removed her sunglasses. Cam didn't react at all to her shiner.

Yeah, thought A.P., thoroughly disgusted now. *This ain't the first time. Should've known.*

He indicated a kitchen chair, Terry wedging his bulk into it without a word. Controlling his fury, A.P. poured himself more coffee, then took the opposite seat. Plucked cigarettes and his Zippo from his shirt pocket. "Smoke?"

"No, thanks."

Cam came bounding into the kitchen, trailing red ribbon and Christmas wrapping paper, carrying what appeared to be a large plastic robot with bristling gears and spikes. "Look, Mom! Look what Terry gave me!"

She turned from her place at the table, moving in slow motion, as if her body would not obey her brain. "Cam, I want you to go on back into the front room there, and don't come out until I tell you. Okay?"

"But Mom…!"

A.P. registered her tension. "You heard her, son."

He disappeared. The TV came to raucous life, unseen.

Mickey got to her feet, shaking her head, making for the sink. "Excuse me, you two. I need some Motrin, Adrien. Don't get up— I know where it is."

But Terry bounded to his feet as she passed and slapped the side of her head. A.P. latched onto his wrist, slow to react out of pure disbelief. "Hey! Hey! What the hell're you *doing*, man?"

He shook free, so nonchalant it was eerie. "Cunt."

A.P. turned. Mickey had made it to the relative safety of the bathroom. He stood.

"I hate it," said Terry, "her playing me off against you this way.

Or playing you off against me. Tell her to come on out here. Stop acting like such a goddam cunt coward."

This is sure one fucked-up salaud here, A.P. marveled. *Higher than a kite, on shit I've probably never even heard of.* He met Mickey in the bathroom doorway, but backed her further inside, right up against the tub. "You okay?"

She nodded.

He lowered his voice. "What's he on? Speed? Cocaine? All of the above?"

"I don't know. Well, steroids, certainly…"

Steroids. "Where do you *meet* these guys, Mick? You cruise the mental institutions?"

She grabbed his elbow, her teeth showing. "What? What? You think I'm *enjoying* this, pal? I told you not to go out there, not to start anything! The only way to settle anything with him is to *talk.* Just *talk* it out with him, and stay real calm."

"*Mais* yeah," he touched her injured face, "I see how well that works."

"Tell that cunt coward to come on out here!"

"Don't argue with him," A.P. told her. "Take Cam next door to the Ryans'."

"And what do *you* plan on doing?"

"Walk him down to the Green Hill Inn for about six Bloody Marys—his, not mine." He looked out of the doorway.

Cam stood just inside the kitchen, picking at a scab.

"Get back in yonder, son, or I'll wear you out right here, I swear to God!" he threatened, suddenly frightened. Positioned between Mickey and Terry, but leaving Cam uncovered. Was Terry a threat to Cam?

"Go to the Ryans'," he instructed Mickey again. "They've probably overheard him already, yelling like a lunatic. They'll be sympathetic."

"I'm not yelling," Terry—eavesdropping—casually objected. "Cunt."

"Stop calling me that," said Mickey. "My son can hear."

A.P. came to the table, pulled out a chair to take a seat,

knowing it was time to start some serious decompression here. "Hey, *podna*—you like Bloody Marys?"

"Cunt."

Mickey emerged from the bathroom, headed for the front room and Cam.

"Cunt!" Terry punched at her, and she dodged. Unharmed.

But it didn't matter, because his mere effort at punching had snapped something essential in A.P.'s self-control. Something popped loose like a catapult, like elastic stretched too far, a spring wound too tight, energy released into two very strong arms in a tenth of a millisecond. They popped loose themselves, jamming the table against Terry's gut, pinning him to the far wall. And then their outraged fingers were in the man's sparse red hair, bringing the attached head crashing face down onto the table top. Coffee geysered.

"Oh my God!" Mickey shrieked. "Oh my God! Oh my God!"

A.P. crashed Terry's face again, while time and surprise were still on his side. Cartilage and bone crunched, blood jetting out of the young man's nose. He tried to do it a third time, but Terry was still conscious. No longer surprised, and his thick neck went rigid.

He shoved A.P. at the refrigerator, head-first.

Mickey was in the way, and received a fist in her stomach. Terry hit her hard. What she cried then was *"Please!"* He hit her again, up near her jaw, almost in her throat. Crush her larynx, she'd suffocate.

A.P. lost his mind, getting Terry up around the neck from behind, attempting to snap his spinal column the way he'd been taught in Basic—*so much for being a good host.*

"What the hell's going on over there?" came the landlord shout through the wall.

Mickey screamed back at the wallboard, *"Call 911! Call 911! Hurry!"* and wrapped her body around her child's.

A.P. didn't possess the footing now to break Terry Lanzl's neck, but he could cut off the bigger man's air supply for a while, riding his back like a parasite, satisfied to squeeze with his hard forearm and watch the back of Terry's ear turning blue right at his own eyelid. *We don't fight clean where I'm from*, podna...

Mickey crouched around Cam like a sheltering tent.

Yet Terry had oxygen reserves, maybe all that air stored in his head. He fought free.

A.P.'s good hand scrabbled blind now for a weapon, a stray fork, a bottle, a kitchen knife.

Terry kicked at his crotch, but A.P.'s dodge sent the blow into the injured hip instead. He fell very hard. The pain was audible. It roared.

Terry kicked him twice in the head to make sure he stayed down. Bones cracked in his face.

I can't get up, he discovered, trying, seeing the hiking boots coming back for him. *Shit, I'm about to get stomped.*

He heard the thudding impact, his own gasps. And tried to curl up like a fetus, but the bad leg wouldn't curl.

"*Stoppit, Terry!*" Mickey was shrieking, flailing at him. "*Don't be crazy! This is crazy!*"

He slapped her down.

Then kicked A.P. in the nape of the neck, then his kidneys. In the bad hip again. Something was loose in the bad hip.

"*Call 911!*" came Mickey's appeals to the landlord wall.

He had one arm over his skull and the other hand over his genitals to ride it out, waiting for the psychopath to take a breather, the opportunity to snag Terry's ankle. He didn't register pain now. His mind was clear.

One more time, fis d'putain. *Come in close enough, and I got your bootlaces. Then we'll have us that talk, while I kneel on your neck.*

Small bare feet appeared suddenly on the hardwood floor right at his eye level. "Freeze!" came Cam's quavery voice somewhere in the air above. "*Freeze!*"

A.P. looked up to see the barrel of his own 9mm Ruger semi-automatic poking into Terry Lanzl's left buttock. Cam had not taken the safety off. He didn't know from safeties. He knew from television.

"*No*, son!" A.P. despaired through busted lips, knowing what would happen.

And it did.

Terry reached down and took the weapon. Cam hadn't expected him to do this. Bad guys didn't do this on TV. They froze on TV, like they were ordered to do.

They're dead right about gun control, thought A.P. as he watched his adversary take the safety off. *Get us out of this, God, I'll vote for every gun control measure that comes down the pike. Fed-Ex my own to the NRA in a box full of cat shit.*

His face was raw meat where his mouth and the insides of his cheeks had been cut by his own teeth. He couldn't see well. A few ribs were out of commission and he couldn't tell anything about the bad hip, except that it wasn't working. But Terry Lanzl—all by himself, whether armed or not—wasn't Viet Cong artillery.

The realization brought him confidence.

Time went into slow motion.

Yeah, he thought, satisfied at the deceleration. *Gives me an edge.*

But it was Cam's crying that got through to him, that finally hurt him. That distracted him now. From someplace against the wall. Where was Mickey?

A.P. rolled over. One eye still worked.

Terry was at the stove, with the gun barrel to Mickey's temple.

"Oh hey—you don't want her brains on you, *podna!*" A.P.'s mouth told Terry of its own accord, on automatic pilot, while his mind and heart jumped all over the place. "She's got HIV—you don't want her blood all over you that way, do you, man? I ought to know, it's *me* that gave it to her. Raping her, while she begged for mercy..."

Terry lowered the weapon but put it to her chest and then belly, testing, crazy, beginning to heave and sob.

"She's a good girl. –An innocent girl, and totally true to you, Terry. Totally. But she's got HIV now, *podna*, think about it." A.P. heard his own mouth spewing out incredible bullshit. His soul shut down. "I've raped her. Twice. You pull that trigger, you'll get it too, all those open wounds on you now. Splash that diseased blood into 'em, you're as good as dead, man..."

"Don't try that shit on me!" Terry blubbered. "Liar!"

"Why you think she wouldn't sleep with you last night? She was *saving your life*, man. Protecting you."

The sirens were coming. A.P. could hear them through the floor boards.

God, let it be for us and not just some fire down the street, he prayed, *just a fire truck on its way to the zoo...*

"Let her go, Terry, just listen—she's a good girl, and Cam needs her, and you'll go to prison, okay? All them queers be on you like white on rice, you hear what I'm saying?"

Terry shook his head.

Mickey didn't seem to be breathing. She stood there in her skirt and Mexican sweater, upon the heels of her Western boots, but no breath moved visibly in or out.

The gun barrel returned to her head, making a depression under her jaw. A.P. calculated the angle a round would travel up into her brain. Understanding finally what that illegal hair trigger he'd installed on this weapon really meant. He *saw*. His heartbeat rocked him. *Hail Mary, full of grace, the Lord is—*

"Terry? Hey, *Terry*? Bet a pretty boy like you'd just love to have them convicts fooling with your tight little ass, wouldn't you?" – *with thee. Blessed art thou among women and blessed is the fruit of thy womb, Jesus he'll kill her when the cops come through the gate, him holding her like that. He might not really intend to, he's acting out some macho-stud TV movie. But he'll kill her by reflex.* "Hey, Terry? That's what's wrong with you, man? You don't like women?"

The pistol wavered. Flicking out from under Mickey's jaw like a snake's head. "*Shut up! You shut up!*"

Point it at your own head, homophobe, do us all a big favor. "Shit, you're just a big ol' closet-queen, Terry, that's why you've got to hit women, man! I got you figured out, I seen the way you keep looking at me." A.P.'s broken mouth laughed. "Want to kiss me, baby? Want to suck my dick, honey?"

The barrel homed in on him now like a negative searchlight. Its hole was black. *Holy Mary*, Mère de Dieu, *pray for us* pauvres maintenant *and at the hour of our death, amen. Hail Mary, full of grace*—

"Hey, Terry? Terry Fairy? You're pathetic, dude, you know that? You're sick, *podna*. Put the weapon down." His pores emitted sweat, despair and crazy joy. "You don't have to hurt any of us. All you need is rehab, *mon ami*."

Terry shook his head, tears dripping off his chin. His gun hand did a wavering jig. "I'm going to jail anyway. For assault and battery. You said."

"Hey, Terry, I ain't seen a thing, man! Tripped over a *maudit* stool and broke my own damn face, far as I'm concerned."

"She's making a big mistake, hooking back up with you, Adrien. I don't want to see her go through it—she's better off dead. She doesn't know what's good for her. You're not good for her."

Where are the fucking cops? How far away from the gate?

"Terry. Hey." *Just don't point it at her again.* "Yeah, I'm slime, I'm trash, I'm the Devil in a Coonass suit, but at least I ain't no big mascara-wearing princess queen like *you*, man, Terry Fairy—you sick fuck, you pathetic joke, the entire NFL's convinced you wear lace pantyhose, you shave with Neet, you put tampons up your ass!"

Purple-faced with wrath, Terry was herky-jerky, in a two-handed shooter's stance now. A.P. could see right up into the shaking tiny black hole where the round would come out.

Yeah, couyon *fuck's going to kill me, right in front of Cam and Mick on Christmas Day, on my own goddam kitchen floor. Which needs sweeping, by the way. As soon as somebody makes a move, I'm gone.*

There were other people in the kitchen now, A.P. noticed. Mean old Papère Robichaux—Feen's father—standing right there behind Mickey and Terry in his sweat-stained fedora and ragged denim, guitar in one hand and whiskey bottle in the other, scowling from beneath black-caterpillar brows. His thin-lipped mouth moved now, in French. "So what'll it be this time, bastard? You coming?"

Do I have to?

Papère spat. "Shit, son, you got a bad concussion, a busted hip, two punctured lungs. What does it take?"

But what'll keep this pote-sac *here from killing the love of my life, if I go now? Because no way I'm letting him kill her. Not if I can help it.*

"Police're almost at the gate." The old man pointed with his bottle. "Pistol's not on automatic, he won't get off more than a single shot…"

A.P. considered that. Remembering: *Mick, I'd take a bullet for you.*

"You and your big mouth, you bastard. Didn't Feen try to teach you fighting don't solve anything?"

Too late for all that now. A.P. looked into the barrel of the gun.

But a small boy suddenly bounded out from behind Papère, in T-shirt and shorts, light-footed on bare soles, wiping both palms on the fabric at his chest. "Um… Knock-knock, A.P.!" He tittered like a bird, grinning up at his grandfather, then back down at his brother. "Guess who?"

Too astonished to feel astonishment, A.P.'s disbelieving eyes began to leak something besides blood. *Is that you, Tee-Nick? Can that really be you, lil' man, little lost Nicholas? How on earth—?*

" 'Must be Saint Nick!' " joked the joyous child, swinging his arms. "Ho ho ho!"

Oh my God. He looks so happy.

Tenderly, tenderly, Tee-Nick reached down, an angel's gesture. "Um… Okay, so here. Take my hand—it's clean. Come with me, I know the way, bro. It's all good. I forgive you and we love each other."

Mais *yes. We do*, thought A.P., looking past him, past the black hole in the barrel to make eye contact with Michelle Wickham, Homecoming Queen, her bruised face, her bloody nose. Little short cheerleader skirt, blond hair like a halo, that remarkable rosy mouth of hers that would kiss him anywhere.

But he wept, because he didn't want to leave her.

"It's time," said Papère. "Police're here."

Y'all wait a sec, A.P. pleaded, *there's something I got to tell her!*

196

"Crazy *couyon* here's reflexes ain't going to wait on nothing—get your say said, *quick*."

Mickey's face was like a light, pink and white. Her blue eyes were a beacon that held him.

He took Tee-Nick's small warm hand, and opened his mouth. "Mick, I love y—"

The gate clanged.

CHAPTER TWENTY-FIVE

Down in Bois Sec, Delphine heard the gunshot.

She was out in her own front yard on Christmas morning, punting a new football to grandsons Troy and Jason, dressed in jeans and Keds and a big plaid lumber-jack shirt. The toe of her little canvas shoe thudded into its target. A child's voice spoke into her ear: "Ho ho ho."

But the only children she could see were in front of her.

The air cracked like a cherry bomb.

She stopped. "Okay, what's with all the funny business?"

"What, Mamère?" asked Troy.

"One of you jokers, I guess. Fire-cracker."

But Troy was on punt return, and he and Jason just shrugged at each other. Nobody at the house back there was showing himself. The *galerie* was empty.

And Delphine suddenly knew what she'd heard, even before she remembered her dream.

She knew what she'd heard, and she knew what it was, and she knew what it meant.

Crossing herself, she fell to her knees right there, right upon the muddy mown weeds, and began to pray like a madwoman, Jason and Troy forgotten.

Too late, assessed her terrified mind, but she wouldn't stop. That statue of Our Lady spreading her hands in blessing over the frozen irises at the foot of her pedestal—Delphine's flooding eyes couldn't go anywhere else but there. Her lips moved: *Hail Mary, full of grace.*

Troy ran for the house.

CHAPTER TWENTY-SIX

The church was full of white flowers.

People came in quietly, and spoke to each other only when they needed to. And then they whispered.

Delphine wore a new navy-blue crepe dress, and Bay-Bay had done her hair for her. She wore eyeshadow, but no mascara. No use in mascara, not if it ended up all over her cheeks like she knew it would.

The immediate family overflowed the first three pews, children squeezed in rows between adults like sparrows on a wire. Delphine heard them stirring and breathing in back of her, her sons and their wives and kids, her daughters and their families. One of Lolo's little girls kept kicking the pew in front of her, and Delphine registered the child's presence—this grand-daughter—this grandchild among so many beautiful grandchildren.

Life renews itself, she thought. *The kids teach us that. Our little birds, flying off into the future.*

Paul sat next to her, with Bay-Bay and Huey at his right. Dangerously quiet, prone to tremors, he had stopped looking anybody in the eye ten minutes ago and cleared his throat a lot. She groped for his hand now, that warm rough palm where the skin felt like concrete. He didn't pull it away.

There were many individuals Delphine didn't recognize in the pews further back, but No-Frills' Kyle and Laskey were there in suits. The Ryan family—A.P.'s landlords—had made it. Mike and Carla Maggio from the record store were back there somewhere. Lamar Legendre and family sat close to the front, with Bee-Bee's wife. Bee-Bee himself was off closeted with the priest right now, supervising everything.

I'll do all right, 'til I see Mickey and Cam, Delphine realized. *Then it's Kleenex time. I'll go to pieces.*

Here's my nightmare, she understood again, soft organ music lulling her senses. *This is my exact dream, all those nightmares I was having last autumn. Here's the tragedy I dreamed about.*

And I couldn't do one damn thing to keep it from happening.

Her eyes leaked, ahead of schedule. Fumbling for tissues, she knocked her purse to the floor in her search. A lipstick rolled across the marble floor, echoing. She sat up straight again, embarrassed, aware of kids kicking the tube like a soccer ball until their moms could stop them.

Mickey's own mother was seated across the aisle with several well-dressed strangers, serene and coiffed, facing straight ahead, in no danger of choking up or becoming teary. Delphine, wounded, ducked her head and knelt on the folded-down cushion.

"Feen?" Paul interrupted her prayer, tobacco-scented breath at her ear. "Get up, babe. It's about to start."

But the flowers and candles up there at the altar threatened to undo her. Bee-Bee Legendre and the priest were up there, watching. That's where A.P. would be.

The organ soared. It was beginning.

Paul took her arm.

People behind her were already getting to their feet with coughs and rustlings, and Delphine stood along with them on numb feet. Her body began to tremble.

"Look back," Paul cued her.

She did.

And Michelle Wickham Savoie was coming down the central aisle over a white carpet runner, veiled, in long ivory satin and lace. On her son Cam's arm.

A black-haired man on crutches waited for them at the altar.

He didn't look like himself—he looked *better* than himself—and Delphine finally attempted a glance up. She paid for it, because the love and pride and awe that constricted her chest also crumpled her chin. Her lower lip wobbled.

Cameras clicked.

Square shoulders filling out the seams of the black tux with a tailored elegance that would've done a prince proud, he looked pretty much the same way he'd always looked, his nose and cheeks healed. He stood relatively straight now, even on these crutches, after a hip replacement. But his eyes were better than they'd ever been. Deeper, compelling. Luminous. Maybe that wasn't all plastic surgery.

The beauty of his face was honed by its expression.

Delphine's self-control evaporated. Hot tears spilled over her lower lids.

"Don't he look *fine?*" Paul whispered. "Even got his *maudit* hair combed."

Yes, A.P. looked fine. *Took him four months to get here, to look this fine*, his mother sniffled. *Took more than just Time, too.*

Took something I don't understand.

"His heart stopped in the ambulance," Mickey had told her. "They lost his pulse. Three blocks away from Baptist Hospital."

"You remember anything, boo?" Delphine had quizzed him, when he was strong enough to entertain de-briefing. When he was beginning to look like himself again, broken jaw wired shut, face and nose healing. With a little gold St. Jude medal around his neck, presented by Kyle, Lamar, and Laskey. St. Jude, patron saint of hopeless cases, lost causes. Who must've been hard at work, because this one was lost no longer.

A.P.'s eyes had begun to watch normal things again, like nephews and television and Bee-Bee Legendre, not just Mickey and Cam and the empty air.

"I saw Tee-Nick, who had me by the hand," he'd said through medically-clenched teeth. "Papère was there, too. But then next thing I remember, Mick had me in her arms and was screaming

'Breathe! Breathe! Breathe!' —and I kept trying, because I knew if I didn't, she'd kill me." *His poor face can't smile all that good yet, but his eyes sure can.*

* * *

Glued to him throughout the whole ordeal, not flying back up to New York even once for clothes or closure, Mickey had slept at the hospital, in his room when they'd allowed her to, living on junk food and reading Walker Percy novels. She hadn't suspected the nature of her own physical situation, those first few days when A.P. was still in critical condition in the ICU and they wouldn't let her spend a whole lot of time with him. Her nausea and vertigo had been chalked up to shock. Her crying jags were not inappropriate.

She'd buttonholed doctors in her hormonal frenzies, threatening them with malpractice lawsuits, poking them in their collarbones exactly the way her late father would've done, until Delphine worried about a possible nervous breakdown.

"See a doctor for yourself, *cher,*" had been her plea. "Do it for Cam. Do it for A.P."

His condition began to stabilize the afternoon Mickey put her lips to his earring and whispered, "We're going to have another baby, my love."

The Hand of God.

* * *

Look at him up there now. Look at how he looks at her.

Look at Bee-Bee, too. Best Man.

"This time next year," Bee-Bee had nodded to Feen the night before at the wedding rehearsal, an uncharacteristically happy grin almost paralyzing his face and mouth, "I be loading my last cargo, depend on it. Saying goodbye to the docks. Come stand right here. See what I see."

"But, Mr. Bee-Bee, you don't represent but one musician," Delphine observed. "And he's still on crutches."

"You understand publicity, Miz Savoie?" He'd pointed to the front pew with an unlit cigar, where A.P. sat playing tic-tac-toe with Cam. "All them news stories? *People* magazine? Phone calls I'm getting now, from big-ass record labels and music clubs in Miami? Fame's what you call it. Get ready.

"Your boy's going to be *big*."

* * *

And Cam? Delphine watched the dutiful child now, escorting his mother down the aisle.

"The boy needs therapy," Mickey's mother had opined last night to anybody that would listen, "and you'd better do it *soon*."

"Stuck-up *cocotte* had no business whoring around with somebody like Lanzl in front of her kid that way in the first place," had been Paul's private contribution. "What a world."

"Cam's going to have nightmares, big time," observed Bay-Bay. "Prepare yourselves, because he's going to wake up hollering every single night for about eight more years…"

So Delphine had finally taken him aside during a lull in the rehearsal, out of the church's wide front doors and into the warm spring night, moonlight making the nearby tombs glow, frogs speaking loud from Bayou Lafourche. The water out there made no noise. It flowed without discernible current, but it flowed.

"So you like being in the wedding, boo?" She accompanied him down the steps, then off the walkway and onto mown grass. Stepping out of her high heels, she registered its green resilience.

"Why do they have to rehearse getting married? They're *already* married."

"It's before God this time, though. Not just in front of a justice of the peace, or some judge. This time it's by a priest. This time it's for keeps."

"Well, good." He reached down, picked up a dead stick and threw it. "Because I sure don't want there to be any more *Terrys*."

"You and me both. Maybe Terry'll get some kind of treatment

now. Locked up like he is. He's got parents who love him. A mom and a dad. Who'd like to see him healthy."

"I think he's *bad*. I hope he goes to prison."

"...Just like your own mom and dad want to see *you* turn out okay." The night air smelled of sweet olive. Silhouetted shrimp boats gleamed on the bayou, their lights lit. "Are you okay, Cam?"

He blew his light bangs out of his face. "Yeah."

"For real?"

"...I have bad dreams..."

She reached down for his hand, but she didn't make him look up at her. And he didn't look up. "I can't talk about it with Mom and Dad, though, Mamère. They worry too much. About me."

"*Mais* yeah," said Delphine. "But some of us know for sure you're okay. Like me. I know for sure."

"Mamère," said Cam, "when you get shot, the bullet makes a little hole in your front. But it makes a great *big* hole in your back. Where it comes out. Bullets don't go all the way through you on TV."

She pulled him against her side. "TV ain't real, boo."

"It was *me* who gave Terry that gun." Cam began to cry.

Delphine stooped hastily, eye to eye with him in the dim light. "*Cher*, you did what you had to do, and it took a lot of bravery, boo. Maybe TV doesn't teach you this either, but a person can die from getting beat up. You can kill a person with a pair of hard-toed hiking boots, and a maniac in them. I think you're a *hero*, me."

Cam sobbed.

"Oh, *cher*, oh, Cam, my dearest child," Delphine held him, "It wasn't no kind of fair fight, your daddy was already hurt. He was hurt a long time ago, before you were even born. Terry was kicking him to death. A few more kicks in the head, he'd have had permanent brain damage. Or would've just died. You gave him a little more time, *tee-boug*. A little bargaining room. Your daddy can do a whole lot with just a little, son."

"But Dad died anyway."

"Who told you that?"

"Newspapers. I just turned eight." He sounded testy. "I can *read!*"

"Boo, some people do die and then come back. We can't explain how it happens. But I do know the chances of coming back're a whole lot better if your skull isn't all stove in..."

"Is 'stove' a French word?"

"*Coo* Lord, I don't know what kind of word 'stove' is. Think I heard it on television."

They both laughed.

Then he pulled away. "But I also saw a good thing, Mamère. My dad saved my mom's life. Did you know that?"

"Yes. She's talked about it. Even Terry's mentioned it, I understand. *People* magazine wrote about it."

"But here's the part I don't get. It was supposed to be his *head*." His brown eyes were very dark in the faint light.

"What?"

"Dad's *head*."

"What about it?"

"The gun was pointed at Dad's *head*," said Cam. "From only about four feet away."

The night became cold. Delphine held him against her and listened to the frogs making love.

He began to cry again. "If that bullet had gone into his *head*, and then made that big hole out of the back of it—"

"But it didn't." She tightened her grip on him. "Terry missed."

"*How?*"

"I... don't know. Nerves. The cops coming. I don't know."

"*How could he miss?*"

"Son, I don't know. Grace of God. Prayers to Our Lady." She crossed herself.

"I keep having these scary dreams, and I dream about a scary old man there in the kitchen with us—this real mean, really scary-looking old man." Cam sniffled. "Hitting Terry's hand with a liquor bottle. His *gun hand*. Spoiling his aim."

Delphine shifted her position. *Mère de Dieu.* "Well, but that's a pretty good bad dream then, isn't it?

He continued to wheeze. "You don't get it. This old dude's *terrifying*. He even scares Dad, in my dreams. Lot more than Terry does."

Delphine felt some emotion she couldn't identify. "When my mother died, I dreamed she turned into a butterfly. And flew off."

"But did she?"

"No."

He moved his head to look up at her face. "How old were you?"

"Real little. Four or five."

"Well, maybe she did fly away. I mean, like her soul."

"Yes."

"My mom says that none of us will sleep enough to dream anyway, once my baby sister gets born."

Delphine smiled. "Yeah."

"And Dad says, 'a sucking chest wound is nature's way of telling you to prioritize.' "

She had to laugh, finally.

"So is that 'astute', Mamère?"

"Extremely."

"He also says something else—but I think it might be dirty, since Mom blushes and laughs at it…"

"*Hush!*"

But Cam was chortling now with delight in the forbidden. "Dad says, 'No physical therapy in the world equals a sincere hand job.' "

"Keep your voice down, boo!" But she laughed.

"So Dad's really alive again, I guess, huh?"

"I imagine if he was any more alive, none of us could stand it."

* * *

Just look at Cam here. She remembered that exchange now, watching him square his small shoulders as he led his mother to the altar. Seeing how very tall he was getting, knowing how very tall he would become, with his mother's genes. Delphine saw the man inside of the boy for an instant now, inside his solemn and dignified carriage, and she wept afresh.

He made eye contact with her as he passed, his eyes ringed with light, the reflection of all those candles amid his blond lashes. But his innocence was gone.

Delphine pressed her eyelids shut.

He'd made it up to the altar rail, to the priest, when she opened them again. Cam took his mother's long pale hand and then placed it into the browner one of his father's. The congregation—at Bee-Bee's signal—sat back down.

In the pew directly behind Delphine, Lolo began to sniffle. Auradele took it up.

Lamar Legendre—at his own electronic keyboards, up front—began playing, then singing *Ave Maria* in a voice so angelic it almost frightened. Mickey's mother, finally, groped for tissues and made a mess of her make-up, thawing like a snow woman.

The vows were spoken, and rings exchanged—A.P. already wore his, in his ear as usual, but Mickey reached up to touch it. When the moment came for them to kneel, Bee-Bee helped him with his crutches and he *knelt*. Without hesitation, in communion with his wife and heaven and all the saints Delphine could not see, but knew for sure that her father and her little Tee-Nick were among. When given the wine, A.P. accepted it fearlessly, as if trusting his sobriety to heaven. Bowing his head like the most grateful of entities.

Most of the congregation became utterly undone, even some of the men. Blown noses honked. Delphine was deeply satisfied. Cameras clicked and whirred like insects. Bay crouched near the front pew, videotaping, a new hand-held video camera pushed up against her eye socket like a telescope.

Most of this equipment, though, belonged to the press. Bee-Bee looked out over the assembly like an impresario, assessing its emotions, counting the house.

Everybody's innocence is gone, Delphine realized, *except for maybe A.P.'s*. His seemed oddly intact to her, even growing. *They all abandoned him, ran away from him and denied him. But he's still here. Resurrected.*

It's like he's Jesus, she thought. —And then instantly repudiated the notion, because it was too sacrilegious to entertain. Yet not easily squelched.

My middle name is Marie.

* * *

Hoopla and uproar!

The traditional wedding reception went into full swing, with all the drunken old Frenchmen pinning the customary cash money onto Mickey's bridal veil in exchange for a waltz, alarm over Auradele's catching of the bouquet, and laughter at uproarious, ribald toasts. There were also tabloid reporters to deflect, with a polite *"Je ne parle pas l'Anglais."*

Delphine collapsed into bed very late that night beside Paul, while Mickey and A.P. flew high above the black Gulf of Mexico aboard a 757 on their way to Cancun for their honeymoon, son Cam asleep between them in the middle seat, their tiny daughter slumbering in utero.

But sleep would not come for Delphine, and she finally gave up on it. Got up without waking Paul, and went to the kitchen for a glass of red wine. The living-room was dark and quiet. She sank down into the rocking chair.

Remembering all those times she'd sat beside Tee-Nick's hospital bed, but not like this, not in peace. She thought about him, a child who the later-born Bobby and Auradele had never known. She thought about Adrien Paul, his birth. His deaths. His children.

She pondered dreams and portents, living and dying and getting old, rain and sun and stars and hurricanes, the wine warming her soul. She recalled what her father had taught her about the ways of the muskrat and the nutria, the simple earthbound mammals that had kept her family alive in those days. She remembered her mother's hands.

She listened to the clock ticking on the mantel, the sound of Paul coughing in the bedroom in his sleep.

"Feen." A.P. had called her over, just before leaving for the airport, taking her hand out there on the *galerie* and putting it to Mickey's belly. "We're naming her 'Nicole'. After Tee-Nick."

No way I can speak.

"With 'Delphine' as her middle name," Mickey had added. "Is that okay with you?"

No way I can speak.

Over the head of Our Lady out there, a monarch butterfly flapped northward.

THE END

The next novel in the *Jolie Blonde* series is

CAJUN SPIRIT.

What they said about CAJUN SPIRIT:

"There's a genuine ghost story here, but it's the human story that sets off shivers."

—*San Francisco Chronicle*

"What lifts Harper's work above the ordinary ghostly romance, beyond its fine use of setting, is the intensity of these characters, their struggles to move on, to make new lives, all the while feeling the pull of the past, the longing to redeem the lost moment."

—*The Times-Picayune*

Or…

Try another beautifully-written M.A. Harper romance:

http://amzn.to/1v9O927

Also by M.A. Harper:

DIAMONDS IN THE SKY

CAJUN LOVE SONG

CAJUN SPIRIT

A Respectful Request

We hope you enjoyed *Fire on the Bayou* and wonder if you'd consider reviewing it on Goodreads, Amazon (http://amzn.to/1vnGhJK), or wherever you purchased it? The author would be most grateful.

How About A Free Book?

Keep up to date on terrific new books, and get a freebie at the same time! First click here to join our mailing list. Next, choose any book you want from the booksBnimble website and drop a note to julieorleans@cox.net letting us know which one to send you. We'll get it to you immediately. **The password is: mailing list.**

Or request a review copy of any book on the booksBnimble website. Just write julieorleans@cox.net and we'll send it right away. The only thing we ask in return is an honest review. **Be sure to say the password:** *review copy.*

Important: Don't forget to tell us whether it's a free sign-up book or a review copy.

About the Author

M. A. HARPER, a southern farmer's daughter, was once a free-lance commercial artist. But upon her discovery that no picture is always worth 1,000 words, she took the 1,000-word option and ran with it. Her published works include novels, children's plays, non-fiction articles and the online FAINT GLOW BLOG. Fascinated by those thin places where reality seems to give way into something Other, she think her fiction can be described as Supernatural Lite. Among past and present pursuits are palmistry, skydiving and metaphysics. A guilty pleasure is NFL football and her day jobs have included shoe seller, New York City window dresser, department store sales clerk and legal office receptionist. Her favorite night job was as off-Off-Broadway stage manager for many productions at La MaMa. She currently lives in New Orleans. If asked to define herself in one word, she'll say "interested".